W9-BOO-526

WITHDRAWN

THE JACK TALES

THE
JACK TALES

Told by R. M. Ward and his kindred in the Beech Mountain section
of western North Carolina and by other descendants of
COUNCIL HARMON (1803–1896) elsewhere in the southern
mountains; with three tales from Wise County, Virginia.

Set down from these sources and edited by RICHARD CHASE;
with an appendix compiled by HERBERT HALPERT;
and illustrated by BERKELEY WILLIAMS, Jr.

HOUGHTON MIFFLIN COMPANY

www.houghtonmifflinbooks.com

Book design by Lisa Diercks
The text of this book is set in Scala.

Hardcover ISBN 0-618-34693-7
Paperback ISBN 0-618-34692-9
LC: 43-012028

Manufactured in the United States of America
QUM 10 9 8 7 6 5 4 3 2 1

❧

To all those older American citizens
from whom I have had the privilege of learning these stories;
and

❧

To young Americans who will find this book.
For Granny Shores said that you would
"surely delight in the old handed-down tales" and
Old Mr. Ward told me, at the start, that it was for your sake
such a book should be made.

PREFACE

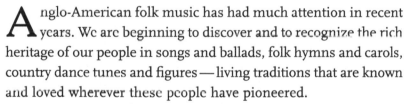

Anglo-American folk music has had much attention in recent years. We are beginning to discover and to recognize the rich heritage of our people in songs and ballads, folk hymns and carols, country dance tunes and figures — living traditions that are known and loved wherever these people have pioneered.

When the great English folklorist, Cecil Sharp,[1] visited Mrs. Jane Gentry in Hot Springs, North Carolina, and recorded sixty English folksongs from her, he came very close to another side of our tradition and he would very probably have taken down this material, too, had he but known that Mrs. Gentry liked to tell what she called "The old Jack and Will and Tom tales." Mr. Sharp asked her only for songs. It remained for Mrs. Isobel Gordon Carter to do the first

---

1. Founder of The English Folk Dance and Song Society in England and the affiliated Country Dance Society in the United States. See also note on page viii and on page 185 in the Appendix.

collecting of The Jack Tales as known to Mrs. Gentry. These tales were published, exactly as Mrs. Gentry told them, in the *Journal of American Folk-Lore* for March 1927. But more of this later.

My own first knowledge of The Jack Tales came in the spring of 1935 through Marshall Ward, a young fellow from western North Carolina. Marshall had heard me talk to a group of teachers about our folksongs.

"I don't know whether you'd be interested or not," he said to me afterward, "but my folks know a lot of old stories that have been handed down from generation to generation like you were saying about the old songs."

"What sort of stories are they?"

"They're mostly about a boy named Jack, and his two brothers, Will and Tom."

"Is that the same boy who climbed a beanstalk?"

"We call that one 'Jack and the Bean Tree.'"

"And did he kill a lot of other giants besides that one up the bean tree?"

"Yes, the time he hired out to the King to clear a patch of new-ground. But we don't tell any of the tales the same way you read them in books."

"Can you tell them?"

"I can; but I don't like to unless there are a lot of kids around."

"Who did you learn them from?"

"From my father and Uncle Mon-roe."

"Where did they learn them?"

"From Old Counce Harmon. He was my great-grandfather."

"How many do they know to tell?"

"About two dozen — Jack Tales and others."

This was the beginning of the long trail.

In time, I visited "Uncle Mon-roe," Mr. R. M. Ward, of Beech Creek, North Carolina, and this book is the result of my chance conversation with Marshall Ward and of many enjoyable days and evenings spent with his "folks" on and near Beech Mountain.

II

R. M. Ward and his people are Southern mountain farmers. Descended from the earliest settlers[2] of that region, one of the most beautiful in the southern Appalachians, they live in the quiet security of a well-established rural economy. They are honest, industrious, and intelligent citizens; and they have rare qualities of kindliness and poise which make them excellent company. On one occasion, both Monroe Ward and his brother Miles stood before a group of distinguished professors, folk-lorists, and musicians at the White Top Folk Festival Conference, and, as much at ease as if they were at their own fireside, fascinated that group of strangers with a number of these tales.

The Ward, Harmon, and Hicks families of Beech Mountain are all fine, hospitable folk, and they have taken a keen interest in our setting down this tradition of theirs for publication. We have heard Jack Tales on all sorts of occasions: sitting on front porches in the evening, sitting on hard clods in the middle of a tobacco patch, leaning in the corner of a rail fence after helping weed the turnips, lounging on hay in the barn, and on cold winter nights sitting up close to blazing logs in great open fireplaces.

One interesting phase of the enjoyment of the tales in that region is a very practical application: that of "keeping the kids on the job" for such communal tasks as stringing beans for canning, or threading them up to make the dried pods called "leather britches." Mrs. R. M. Ward tells us: "We would all get down around a sheet full of dry beans and start in to shelling 'em. Mon-roe would tell the kids one of them tales and they'd work for life!"

---

2. For an account of the ancestry of the Southern mountain people see: "Our Southern Highlanders," by Horace Kephart (New York: Macmillan, 1922), and "The Southern Highlander and His Homeland," by John C. Campbell (New York: The Russell Sage Foundation, 1921). See also the Introduction to Cecil J. Sharp's "English Folk Songs from the Southern Appalachians" (two volumes, edited by Maud Karpeles, London, Oxford University Press, Humphrey Milford, 1932) for an excellent account of the cultural traditions of this region.

This use of the tales seems to be a common custom in that neighborhood where everyone knows about "Jack" and where many others besides "Old Mon-roe" like to try their hand at telling about that boy's scrapes and adventures. It is through this natural oral process that our Appalachian giant-killer has acquired the easygoing, unpretentious rural American manners that make him so different from his English cousin, the cocksure, dashing young hero of the "fairy" tale.

Through the memories of some of his kinsmen we have been given vivid glimpses of "Old Council" Harmon, who was, as far back as we can trace, the chief source of this cycle. His delight in "worldly" things seems to have given much concern to some of his more somber church brethren.

Smith Harmon, the postmaster at Beech Creek, told us: "Old Counce sure did like to have a good time. When he was younger he'd get read out of church ever' now and then. He'd behave for a while, and not make music, or dance, or sing any love songs.[3] But seemed like he loved the old music[4] so much he'd bust out again and get the church folks down on him once more. When he got to be an old man, though, they didn't pay him much mind."

Monroe Ward has told us: "Old Counce was a sight to dance. He was just as good a church member as any of 'em, but he just couldn't stand[5] music. Time anybody would start in picking on the banjo, he 'uld hit the floor;[6] hit didn't differ even if he was in church. Seventy years old, he could clog and buck-dance just as good as a boy sixteen. He knowed how to run reels,[7] too. They didn't dance back then like they do now. They had reels — four-

---

3. "love songs": usually mean traditional ballads.
4. "the old music": generally means our folk music.
5. "couldn't stand": that is, couldn't resist.
6. "hit the floor": jump out of his chair and start dancing a jig.
7. "reels": traditional figure-dances.

handed reels and eight-handed reels. They'd get a set[8] on the floor and some not knowing much about it, they 'uld get bothered up, till Old Counce would get in it and he'd straighten 'em out and get 'em a-goin' again. But ever' time he took part in any such goin's-on somebody would tell it on him and the next Sunday the preacher'd get after *him* again."

With children, however, there was a different outlook.

Miles Ward has given us this account: "Ever-when I'd see Old Counce a-coming, I'd run to meet him so I could walk with him back to the house. Then he'd sit and take me up on his lap, and I'd ask him right off for a Jack Tale. He'd tell me one, too: never did fail me. He loved to tell about Jack."

Monroe Ward is close to his grandfather in his love of fun: as his neighbors have often said to me, "Law, Monroe sure is antick, now, ain't he?"

At first it seemed that The Jack Tales were known only to these Beech Mountain folk and to other descendants of Council Harmon. Wherever Jack Tales turned up, the trail led back to Wautauga County and "Old Counce" Harmon. It was two years after I had seen the issue of the *Journal of American Folk-Lore* containing Mrs. Jane Gentry's versions of The Jack Tales that I learned through her daughter, Mrs. Grover Long, of Hot Springs, how Mrs. Gentry had learned the tales from her grandfather, Council Harmon. Mrs. Long, by the way, also knows many of the tales and tells them delightfully.

Another descendant, Mr. Sam Harmon, now deceased, was found in Tennessee. Several Jack Tales were recorded from him by Mr. Herbert Halpert.

But we have recently found two Jack Tales in the family tradi-

---

8. "set": the formation of a given country dance; for example, square for four couples, longways for six couples (as in the Virginia Reel), round for twelve couples and so on.

tion of Mrs. D. W. Lethcoe, of Damascus, Virginia; and in Wise County, Virginia, we have found three tales unknown to the Wards: "Jack and the Bull," through Mr. James Taylor Adams, of Big Laurel, and recorded from Mrs. Polly Johnson, of Wise; "Jack and King Marock," recorded from Mrs. Nancy Shores, of Pound; and "Soldier Jack," recorded from Gaines Kilgore, of Pound. And, very recently, a Jack Tale was found in Charlottesville, Virginia.

Miss Elizabeth Eggleston, of Hampden-Sydney, Virginia, has told us of Kentucky versions of two of the Wards' tales, known to Mrs. Sally Middleton, of Martin's Fork, in Harlan County. The existence of these other Jack Tales would indicate that they might be more common than we have yet realized. Certainly these tales, as separate units if not as a cycle, must once have been quite commonly known here in America.

It has not been possible for me to explore even all the known sources before the printing of this book. It may be that the publication of The Jack Tales will bring to light many other such stories known by word of mouth in other parts of America, or new elements belonging to some of these present tales, and that all these materials can be incorporated into another work.

III

In reading these stories, it must be kept constantly in mind that this is an oral tradition. The Jack Tales are told, not read, by these people from whom we have recorded them. No two individuals in Beech Mountain section ever tell the same story exactly alike; nor does the same man ever tell any one tale quite the same twice over. Both Mr. Ward and Mrs. Long say that they never retell any tale just the same way. This is, of course, a part of the story-teller's art.

Monroe says, "I allers try to tell 'em the old way, but I har-rdly ever use jest ex-actly the same wor-rds."

Monroe Ward delights in varying the details of a story, especially the give-and-take of dialogue. His brother, Miles, has incorporated several tales[9] into one which he calls "Jack's Travels." On the occasion when we first heard this, Miles stretched it out to last about two hours.

In editing these stories, we have taken the advice of our informants, and the publisher, and retold them, in part, for this business of getting them into print. We have taken the best of many tellings and correlated the best of all material collected into one complete version. The dialect has been changed enough to avoid confusion to the reading eye; the idiom has been kept throughout.

Additions or omissions of any important element in any tale are accounted for in the Appendix, where also will be found other points of particular interest that concern each tale.

We pass on this suggestion, based on the advice and the actual practice of our informants, to those parents who find this book and want to enjoy The Jack Tales with their children: Try to tell them without the book. After you have got the drift of any tale, forget the printed page, and tell it as you please.

Young people who learn or read these tales will not need this advice. They will discover "Jack" and all the other "kids" in the neighborhood will hear about him — under the apple tree in the yard, out on the front porch steps, down at the swimming hole, or walking to and from school.

For all true folk traditions have this dynamic appeal. They stick with us, and they grow and change with every individual who receives them. Setting such things down in cold print is, really, a hazardous undertaking. They do not exist in any book. The old Scottish woman did well to warn Sir Walter that if he printed her ballad it would "never be sung mair."

It is only when our old songs and old tales are passing from one human being to another, by word of mouth, that they can

---

9. Plus "Gulliver's Travels"! Not from oral tradition, however; for Monroe told us, "Miles got that part out of a book I lent him."

attain their full fascination. No printed page can create this spell. It is the living word — the sung ballad and the told tale — that holds our attention and reaches our hearts.

We have not all had grandfathers like Council Harmon, and yet we can, as we rediscover these things, learn them from books; but no one has ever really enjoyed traditional tales fully until he can tell them "by heart" and with no thought but of the telling and of the faces of his listeners.

IV

Most notable about The Jack Tales is their cycle form: It is always through the "little feller" *Jack* that we participate in the dreams, desires, ambitions, and experiences of a whole people. His fantastic adventures arise often enough among the commonplaces of existence, and he always returns to the everyday life of these farm people of whom he is one. There is nothing fantastic about *Jack* himself, even though he is many times aided by forces as mysterious as those with which he contends. In the series of these tales he meets and conquers, in his way, all the varied, real, and imaginary enemies of a highly spiritual folk, never heroic, but always ready and willing in a modest, dryly gay fashion.

Folk prosody rarely has presented so well-rounded a figure as *Jack. Reynard* is a one-sided rogue, the heroes of European collections of tales are many; other central characters are supermen or gods. *Br'er Rabbit*[10] seems to be the only one who shows many

---

10. However, Martha Warren Beckwith says in a recent letter: "It it the cycle form [of The Jack Tales] that is interesting and their appearing among the whites of this country where so little European story has been collected except among the blacks.

"The 'Jack' hero is thoroughly European. If you think of the English tales with which we are most familiar you will recall 'Jack the Giant Killer' and 'Jack and the Beanstalk,' both of which appear in your collection. Jacobs's collection of English tales has other less familiar 'Jack' stories. 'Jack' is in fact an equivalent

facets of character in a connected series of stories. *Jack,* however, is thoroughly human, the unassuming representative of a very large part of the American people.

One clear indication of the great age of this particular family tradition is the appearance in two of their tales of a figure much like the god Woden, in his aspect as The Wanderer, Old Graybeard, The Stranger who helps adventurers in their need. Mysterious, prescient, with a magic staff in his hand, he helps Jack as he once helped Sigurd in the ages before English was spoken here in the mountains of this new land.

v

So many people have had a hand in the making of this book that it would be difficult to account for them all. John Powell's interest and encouragement really kept me going when I wasn't sure that *Jack* would ever find the right publisher. Both he and Mrs. Powell gave sound advice on many points. Martha Warren Beckwith and Doctor Stith Thompson helped with good letters of advice and information. Mrs. Isobel Gordon Carter wrote me about her knowledge of Mrs. Jane Gentry and about her experiences with our folktales. Berkeley Williams, Jr., made trips with me to Beech Mountain and helped in the editing of several difficult places in the Preface and in the tales. The boys and girls of Virginia's 4-H Clubs, at the State Short Course, made excellent listeners when I told my editing of certain tales to them. I am also indebted to Mrs.

---

figure in European story to Brer Rabbit of American Negro or Spider of Jamaican story. That is, he is the trickster hero who overcomes through quick wit or cunning rather than by physical force. He is often aided in European stories by a supernatural helper, 'Hans' is the German form and you will find the name common to French and Spanish stories in the form of the name in those languages. I think you will find a Jack cycle in Spanish-American stories collected in the Texas Folklore Society publications. European folktales told in Jamaica make 'Jack' the hero unless, like the Irish, they invent a fancy name."

Annabel Morris Buchanan, who let me use recordings of several Jack Tales which she set down from Mr. Ward's telling.

All those from whom the tales were collected are fully accounted for in the Appendix.

Katherine Chase, my wife, helped collect some of the tales and it was she who typed them all into a neat manuscript.

And Anne Gay Chase, our twelve-year-old daughter, helped with her own knowledge of folktales and fairy tales which she has been reading since she was seven.

VI

One of the most interesting results of telling these *Jack Tales* is that people ask if I have heard a tale they know. One of my hopes, in seeing this collection published, has been that Americans old and young, who know any such old tales, *Jack Tales* or others, by word of mouth (not out of books) that have been handed down in a family or a neighborhood, would write to me about them. Useful information received would be gratefully acknowledged and incorporated in future work the author hopes to do.

R.C.

PROFFIT, VIRGINIA

January 1943

CONTENTS

THE JACK TALES

To whom it may concern as to the Jack tales and others told By R. M. Ward of Wautauga county in state of N C — P o   Beech Creek I did learn the most of these tales from Council Harmon my mother's daddy in the year of 1886 and 87 and 88 and he was about 80 or 85 years old when I learned the tales from him He was very lively and funny and always had a good time with us children   he told me he learned the tales from his grandfather and he said the tales was learned from the Early settlers of the United States   Council Harmon was married twice and had seven children By his first wife   he had eight children by his last wife Council Harmon was a farmer and did work a farm as long as he was able to work and after he quit farming he came to our house and Did stay with us about 5 years and he told us these tales at night

R. M. Ward

August 20, 1938

R. MONROE WARD

APRIL 1875–NOVEMBER 1944

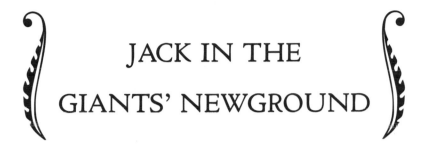

JACK IN THE
GIANTS' NEWGROUND

O ne time away back years ago there was a boy named Jack. He and his folks lived off in the mountains somewhere and they were awful poor, just didn't have a thing. Jack had two brothers, Will and Tom, and they are in some of the Jack Tales, but this one I'm fixin' to tell you now, there's mostly just Jack in it.

Jack was awful lazy sometimes, just wouldn't do ary lick of work. His mother and his daddy kept tryin' to get him to help, but they couldn't do a thing with him when he took a lazy spell.

Well, Jack decided one time he'd pull out from there and try his luck in some other section of the country. So his mother fixed him up a little snack of dinner, and he put on his old raggedy hat and lit out.

Jack walked on, walked on. He eat his snack 'fore he'd gone very far. Sun commenced to get awful hot. He traveled on, traveled on, till he was plumb out of the settle-ment what he knowed. Hit got to be about twelve, sun just a-beatin' down, and Jack started gettin' hungry again.

He came to a fine smooth road directly, decided he'd take that, see where it went, what kind of folks lived on it. He went on, went on, and pretty soon he came to a big fine stone house up above the road. Jack stopped. He never had seen such a big house as that before. Then he looked at the gate and saw it was made out of gold. Well, Jack 'lowed some well-doin' folks must live there, wondered whether or no they'd give him his dinner. Stepped back from the gate, hollered, "Hello!"

A man came to the door, says, "Hello, stranger. What'll ye have?"

"I'm a-lookin' for a job of work."

"Don't know as I need to hire anybody right now. What's your name?"

"Name's Jack."

"Come on up, Jack, and sit a spell. Ain't it pretty hot walkin'?"

"Pretty hot," says Jack.

"Come on up on the porch and cool off. You're not in no hurry, are ye?"

Jack says, "Well, I'll stop a little while, I reckon."

Shoved back that gold gate and marched on in. The man reached in the door and pulled out a couple of chairs. Jack took one and they leaned back, commenced smokin'. Directly Jack says to that man, "What did you say your name was, mister?"

"Why, Jack, I'm the King."

"Well, now, King," says Jack, "hit looks like you'd be a-needin' somebody with all your land. I bet you got a heap of land to work."

"Are ye a hard worker, Jack?"

"Oh, I'm the workin'est one of all back home yonder."

"You a good hand to plow?"

"Yes sir!"

"Can ye clear newground?"

"Why, that's all I ever done back home."

"Can ye kill giants?"

"Huh?" says Jack, and he dropped his pipe. Picked it up, says, "Well, I reckon I could try."

The old King sort of looked at Jack and how little he was, says, "Well, now, Jack, I have got a little piece of newground I been tryin' for the longest to get cleared. The trouble is there's a gang of giants live over in the next holler, been disputin' with me about the claim. They kill ever' Englishman goes up there, kill 'em and eat 'em. I reckon I've done hired about a dozen men claimed to be giantkillers, but the giants killed them, ever' last one."

"Are these here giants very big 'uns?" says Jack.

"Well, they're all about six times the size of a natural man, and there's five of 'em. The old man has got four heads and his old woman has got two. The oldest boy has got two heads, and there's a set of twins has got three heads a-piece."

Jack didn't say nothin', just kept studyin' about how hungry he was.

King says, "Think ye can clear that patch, Jack?"

"Why, sure!" says Jack. "All I can do is get killed, or kill them, one."

"All right, son. We'll make arrange-ments about the work after we eat. I expect my old woman's about got dinner ready now. Let's us go on in to the table."

"Thank ye, King," says Jack. "I hope it won't put ye out none."

"Why, no," says the King. "Hit ain't much, but you're welcome to what we got."

Well, Jack eat about all the dinner he could hold, but the King's old woman kept on pilin' up his plate till he was plumb foundered. His dish set there stacked up with chicken and cornbread and beans and greens and pie and cake, and the Queen had done poured him milk for the third time. The old King kept right on, and Jack didn't want them to think he couldn't eat as much as anybody else, so directly he reached down and took hold on the old leather apron he had on and doubled that up under his coat. Then he'd make like he was takin' a bite, but he'd slip it down in that leather apron. He poured about four glasses of milk down there, too. Had to fasten his belt down on it so's it 'uld hold.

Well, directly the King pushed his chair back, and then he and

Jack went on out and sat down again, leaned back against the house and lit their pipes.

King says to Jack, says, "If you get that patch cleared, Jack, I'll pay ye a thousand dollars a-piece for ever' giant's head you bring down, and pay ye good wages for gettin' that patch cleared: ten cents a hour."

Jack said that suited him all right, and he got the King to point him out which ridge it was. Then Jack says to the King, "You say them giants live over in the other holler?"

King said they did.

Jack says, "Can they hear ye when ye start hackin'?"

"They sure can," says the King.

Jack didn't say nothin'.

The King says to him, "You don't feel uneasy now, do ye, Jack?"

"Why, no, bedads!" says Jack. "Why, I may be the very giantkiller you been lookin' for. I may not kill all of 'em today, but I'll try to get a start anyhow."

So the King told him maybe he'd better go on to work. Said for him to go on out past the woodpile and get him a axe, says, "You might get in a lick or two 'fore them giants come. You'll find a tree up there where them other men have knocked a couple of chips out'n. You can just start in on that same tree."

So Jack started on out to the woodpile. The King watched him, saw him lean over and pick up a little old Tommy hatchet, says, "Hey, Jack! You'll need the axe, won't ye?"

"Why, no," says Jack. "This here'll do me all right." He started on off, turned around, says, "I'll be back about time for supper."

The old King just grinned and let him go on.

When Jack fin'ly got up on that ridge, he was scared to death. He sat down on a log and studied awhile. He knowed if he started in cuttin', them giants would come up there; and he knowed if he didn't, the King 'uld know he hadn't done no work and he'd likely get fired and wouldn't get no supper. So Jack thought about it some more, then he picked out the tallest poplar he could see, and cloomb up in it, started in choppin' on the limbs way up at the very top . . .

Hack! Hack! Hack!

Heard a racket directly, sounded like a horse comin' up through the bresh. Jack looked down the holler, saw a man about thirty foot high comin' a-stompin' up the mountain, steppin' right over the laurel bushes and the rock-clifts. Jack was so scared he like to slipped his hold.

The old giant came on up, looked around till he fin'ly saw where Jack was settin', came over there under him, says, "Hello, stranger."

"Howdy do, daddy."

"What in the world you a-doin' up there?"

"I'm a-clearin' newground for that man lives back down yonder."

"Clearin' land? Well, I never seen such a fool business, start in clearin' newground in the top of a tree! Ain't ye got no sense?"

"Why, that's allus the way we start in clearin' back home."

"What's your name, son?"

"My name's Jack."

"Well, you look-a-here, Jack. This patch of land is ours and we don't aim to have it cleared. We done told the King so."

"Oh, well, then," says Jack, "I didn't know that. If I'd 'a knowed that I'd 'a not started."

"Come on down, Jack. I'll take ye home for supper."

Didn't think Jack 'uld know what he meant. Jack hollered back, says, "All right, daddy. I'll be right down."

Jack cloomb down a ways, got on a limb right over the old giant's head, started in talkin' to him, says, "Daddy, they tell me giants are awful stout. Is that so?"

"Well, some," says the old giant. "I can carry a thousand men before me."

"Well, now, daddy, I bet I can do somethin' you can't do."

"What's that, Jack?"

"Squeeze milk out'n a flint rock."

"I don't believe ye."

"You throw me up a flint rock here and I'll show ye."

So while the old giant hunted him up a flint rock, Jack took his knife and punched a little hole in that old leather apron. The giant chunked the rock up to him and Jack squeezed down on it, pushed up against his apron, and the milk commenced to dreen out . . .

Dreep, dreep, dreep.

"Do it again, Jack!"

So Jack pushed right hard that time, and hit just went like milkin' a cow.

The old giant hollered up to Jack, says, "Throw me down that rock."

He took the rock and squeezed and squeezed till fin'ly he got so mad he mashed down on it and they tell me he crumbled that flint rock plumb to powder.

Then Jack hollered down to him again, says, "I can do somethin' else you can't do."

"What's that, Jack?"

"I can cut myself wide open and sew it back up. And it won't hurt me none."

"Aw, shucks, Jack. I know you're lyin' now."

"You want to see me do it?"

"Go ahead."

Jack took his knife and ripped open that leather apron, took a piece of string he had, punched some holes, and sewed it back up, says, "See, daddy? I'm just as good as I ever was."

Well, the old giant just couldn't stand to let Jack out-do him, so he hollered up, says, "Hand here the knife, Jack."

Took Jack's knife and cut himself wide open, staggered around a little and fin'ly querled over on the ground dead. Well, Jack, he scaled down the tree and cut off the old giant's heads with that little Tommy hatchet, took 'em on back to the King's house.

II

The King paid Jack two thousand dollars like he said he would. Jack eat him a big supper and stayed the night. Next mornin', after he eat his breakfast, Jack told the King he reckoned he'd have to be a-gettin' on back home. Said his daddy would be a-needin' him settin' out tobacco.

But the King says, "Oh, no, Jack. Why, you're the best giant-killer I ever hired. There's some more of that giant gang yet, and I'd like awful well to get shet of the whole crowd of 'em."

Jack didn't want to do it. He figgered he'd done made him enough money to last him awhile, and he didn't want to get mixed up with them giants any more'n he could help. But the King kept on after him till Jack saw he couldn't get out of it very handy. So he went and got the Tommy hatchet, started on up to the newground again.

Jack hadn't hardly got up there that time 'fore he heard somethin' comin' up the holler stompin' and breakin' bresh, makin' the awfulest racket. He started to climb him a tree like he done before, but the racket was gettin' closer and closer, and Jack looked and saw it was them twin giants that had three heads a-piece. Jack looked up, saw them six heads a-comin' over the tree tops, says, "Law me! I can't stand that! I'll hide!"

He saw a big holler log down the hill a ways, grabbed him up a shirt-tail full of rocks and shot in that log like a ground squirrel. Hit was pretty big inside there. Jack could turn right around in it.

The old giants fin'ly got there. Jack heard one of 'em say to the other'n, "Law! Look a-yonder! Somebody's done killed brother."

"Law, yes! Now, who you reckon could 'a done that? Why, he

could 'a carried a thousand Englishmen before him, single-handed.
I didn't hear no racket up here yesterday, did you?"

"Why, no, and the ground ain't trompled none, neither. Who
in the world you reckon could 'a done it?"

Well, they mourned over him awhile, then they 'lowed they'd
have to take him on down and fix up a buryin'. So they got hold on
him, one by the hands and the other by the feet, started on down.

"Poor brother!" says one of 'em. "If we knowed who it was killed
him, we'd sure fix them!"

The other'n stopped all at once, says, "Hold on a minute. There
ain't a stick of wood to the house. Mother sent us up here after
wood; we sure better not forget that. We'll have to have plenty of
wood too, settin' up with brother tonight."

"We better get about the handiest thing we can find," says the
other'n. "Look yonder at that holler log. Suppose'n we take that
down."

Well, they laid the old dead giant down across the top of that
log and shouldered it up. Jack got shook around right considerable inside the log, but after he got settled again, he looked and
saw the old giant in front had the log restin' right betwixt his shoulders. And directly Jack happened to recollect he had all them rocks.
So after they'd done gone down the holler a little piece, Jack he
picked him out a rock and cut-drive at the giant in front—fumped
him right in the back of the head. Old giant stumbled, and stopped
and hollered back at his brother, says, "You look-a-here! What you
a-throwin' rocks at me for?"

"I never so throwed no rocks at you."

"You did so! You nearly knocked me down!"

"Why, I never done it!"

They argued awhile, fin'ly started on down again.

Jack waited a minute or two, then he cut loose with another
good-sized rock. *Wham!*

"You con-founded thing! You've done hit me again!"

"I never done no such a thing!"

"You did too!"

"I never teched ye!"

"You're the very one. You needn't try to lie out of it neither. You can see as good as I can there ain't nobody else around here to throw no rocks. You just hit me one other time now, and I'll come back there and smack the fire out-a you!"

They jawed and cussed a right smart while till fin'ly they quit and got started on down again.

Well, this time Jack picked out the sharpest-edged rock he had, drew back and clipped him again right in the same place. *Pow!* The old giant in front hollered so loud you could 'a heard him five miles, throwed that log off'n his shoulder and just made for the other'n, says, "That makes three times you've done rocked me! And you'll just take a beatin' from me now or know I can't do it!"

Them twin giants started in to fightin' like horses kickin'. Beat any fightin' ever was seen: pinchin' and bitin' and kickin' and maulin' one another; made a noise like splittin' rails. They fit and scratched and scratched and fit till they couldn't stand up no more. Got to tumblin' around on the ground, knockin' down trees and a-kickin' up rocks and dirt. They were clinched so tight couldn't neither one break loose from the other'n, and directly they were so wore out they just lay there all tangled up in a pile, both of 'em pantin' for breath.

So when Jack saw there wasn't no danger in 'em, he crawled out from that log and chopped off their heads, put 'em in a sack and pulled on back to the King's house.

III

Well, the old King paid Jack six thousand dollars for that load of heads. Then Jack said he just had to get on in home. Said his folks would be uneasy about him, and besides that they couldn't get the work done up unless he was there.

But the King says to him, says, "Why, Jack, there ain't but two more of 'em now. You kill them for me and that'll wind 'em up. Then we won't have no trouble at all about that newground."

Jack said he'd see what he could do: went on back that same evenin'.

This time Jack didn't climb no tree or nothin'. Went to work makin' him a bresh pile, made all the racket he could. The old four-headed giant come a-tearin' up there in no time. Looked around, saw the other giants lyin' there dead, came over to where Jack was, says, "Hello, stranger."

"Hello, yourself."

"What's your name, buddy?"

"My name's Jack — Mister Jack."

"Well, Mister Jack, can you tell me how come all my boys layin' here dead?"

"Yes, bedads, I can tell ye," says Jack. "They came up here cussin' and 'busin' me, and I had to haul off and kill 'em. You just try and sass me ary bit now, and I'll kill you too!"

"Oh pray, Jack, don't do that! There's only me and the old woman left now, and she's got to have somebody to get in her stovewood and tote up water."

"You better be careful what ye say then. I ain't goin' to take nothin' off nobody."

"Well, now, I don't want to have no racket with ye at all, Mister Jack. You come on down and stay the night with us, help set up with our dead folks, and we'll get fixed to have a buryin' tomorrow."

"Well, I'll go," says Jack, "but you sure better watch out what you say."

"Oh, I'll not say nothin'," says the old giant. Says, "Law, Jack, you must be the awfulest man!"

So the old giant stuck the dead 'uns under his arm and he and Jack started on down. When they got close to the house, the giant stopped, says to Jack, "Now, Jack, you better wait till I go and tell the old lady you've come down for supper. She might cut a shine. She'll be mad enough already about her boys bein' killed."

He went on in and shut the door. Jack slipped up and laid his ear to the keyhole so's he could hear what they said. Heard him tell his old lady, says, "I've got Jack here, claims to be a giantkiller. I found the boys up yonder at the newground with their heads cut off, and this here Jack says he's the one done it."

The old woman just carried on. Fin'ly the old giant got her hushed, says, "He don't look to me like he's so stout as all that. We'll have to test him out a little, and see whe'er he's as bad as he claims he is."

Directly Jack heard him a-comin' to the door rattlin' buckets. So he stepped back from the house and made like he was just comin' up. The old giant came on out, says, "There ain't a bit of water up, Jack. The old woman wants you and me to tote her some from the creek."

Jack saw he had four piggins big as wash tubs, had rope bails fixed on 'em, had 'em slung on one arm. So they went on down to the creek and the old giant set the piggins down. Stove his two in, got 'em full and started on back. Jack knowed he couldn't even tip one of them things over and hit empty. So he left his two piggins a-layin' there, waded out in the creek and started rollin' up his sleeves. The old giant stopped and looked back, saw Jack spit in his hands and start feelin' around under the water.

"What in the world ye fixin' to do, Jack?"

"Well, daddy," says Jack, "just as soon as I can find a place to ketch a hold, I'm a-goin' to take the creek back up there closer to the house where your old woman can get her water everwhen she wants it."

"Oh, no, Jack! Not take the creek back. Hit'll ruin my cornfield. And besides that, my old lady's gettin' sort-a shaky on her feet; she might fall in and get drownded."

"Well, then," says Jack, "I can't be a-wastin' my time takin' back them two little bitty bucketfulls. Why, I'd not want to be seen totin' such little buckets as them."

"Just leave 'em there, then, Jack. Come on, let's go back to the house. Mind, now, you come on here and leave the creek there where it's at."

When they got back, he told his old woman what Jack had said. Says, "Why, Law me! I had a time gettin' him to leave that creek alone."

He came on out again, told Jack supper wasn't ready yet, said for him to come on and they'd play pitch-crowbar till it was time to eat. They went on down to the level field, the old giant picked up a crowbar from the fence corner. Hit must 'a weighed about a thousand pounds. Says, "Now, Jack, we'll see who can pitch this crowbar the furthest. That's a game me and the boys used to play."

So he heaved it up, pitched it about a hundred yards, says, "You run get it now, Jack. See can you pitch it back here to where I'm at."

Jack ran to where it fell, reached down and took hold on it. Looked up 'way past the old giant, put his hand up to his mouth, hollers, "Hey, Uncle! Hey, Uncle!"

The old giant looked all around, says, "What you callin' me Uncle for?"

"I ain't callin' you. — Hey! *Uncle!*"

"Who are ye hollerin' at, Jack?"

"Why, I got a uncle over in Virginia," says Jack. "He's a blacksmith and this old crowbar would be the very thing for him to make up into horseshoes. Iron's mighty scarce over there. I thought I'd just pitch this out there to him. — Hey! UNCLE!"

"Oh, no, Jack. I need that crowbar. Pray don't pitch it over in Virginia."

"Well, now," says Jack, "I can't be bothered with pitchin' it back there just to where you are. If I can't pitch it where I want, I'll not pitch it at all."

"Leave it layin' then, Jack. Come on, let's go back to the house. — You turn loose of my crowbar now."

They got back, the giant went in and told his old woman he couldn't find out nothin' about Jack. Said for her to test him awhile herself. Says, "I'll go after firewood. You see can't you get him in the oven against I get back, so's we can eat."

Went on out, says to Jack, "I got to go get a turn of wood, Jack. You can go on in the house and get ready for supper."

Jack went on in, looked around, didn't see a thing cookin', and there set a big old-fashioned clay oven with red-hot coals all across it, and the lid layin' to one side.

The old giant lady came at him, had a wash rag in one hand and a comb in the other'n, says, "Come here now, Jacky. Let me wash ye and comb ye for supper."

"You're no need to bother," says Jack. "I can wash."

"Aw, Jack. I allus did wash my own boys before supper. I just want to treat ye like one of my boys."

"Thank ye, m'am, but I gen'ally wash and comb myself."

"Aw, please, Jack. You let me wash ye a little now, and comb your head. Come on, Jacky, set up here on this shelf so's I won't have to stoop over."

Jack looked and saw that shelf was right on one side of the big dirt oven. He cloomb on up on the scaffle, rockled and reeled this-a-way and that-a-way. The old woman kept tryin' to get at him with the rag and comb, but Jack kept on teeterin' around till he slipped off on the wrong side. He cloomb back up and he'd rockle and reel some more. The old woman told him, says, "Sit straight now, Jack. Lean over this way a little. Sakes alive! Don't ye know how to sit up on a shelf?"

"I never tried sittin' on such a board before," says Jack. "I don't know how you mean."

"You get down from there a minute. I reckon I'll have to show ye."

She started to climb up there on the scaffle, says, "You put your shoulder under it, Jack. I'm mighty heavy and I'm liable to break it down."

Jack put his shoulder under the far end, and when the old woman went to turn around and sit, Jack shoved up right quick, fetched her spang in the oven. Grabbed him up a hand-spike and prized the lid on. Then he went and hid behind the door.

Old giant came in directly. Heard somethin' in the oven just a-crackin' and a-poppin'.

"Old woman! Hey, old woman! Jack's a-burnin'."

When she didn't answer, the old giant fin'ly lifted the lid off and there was his old lady just about baked done, says, "Well, I'll be confounded! That's not Jack!"

Jack stepped out from behind the door, says, "No, hit sure ain't. And you better mind out or I'll put you in there too."

"Oh, pray, Jack, don't put me in there. You got us licked, Jack. I'm the only one left now, and I reckon I better just leave this country for good. Now, you help me get out of here, Jack, and I'll go off to some other place and I'll promise not to never come back here no more."

"I'd sure like to help ye, daddy, but I don't think we got time now. Hit's too late."

"Too late? Why, how come, Jack?"

"The King told me he was goin' to send a army of two thousand men down here to kill ye this very day. They ought to be here any minute now."

"Two thousand! That many will kill me sure. Law, what'll I do? Pray, Jack, hide me somewhere."

Jack saw a big chest there in the house, told the old giant to jump in that. Time he got in it and Jack fastened the lid down on him, Jack ran to the window and made-out like that army was a-comin' down the holler, says, "Yonder they come, daddy. Looks to me like about three thousand. I'll try to keep 'em off, though. You keep right still now and I'll do my best not to let 'em get ye."

Jack ran outside the house and commenced makin' a terrible racket, bangin' a stick on the walls, rattlin' the windows, shoutin' and a-hollerin', a-makin'-out like he was a whole army. Fin'ly he ran back in the house, knocked over the table and two or three chairs, says, "You quit that now and get on out of here! I done killed that old giant! No use in you a-breakin' up them chairs. He ain't here I tell ye!"

Then Jack 'uld tumble over some more chairs and throw the dishes around considerable, says, "You all leave them things alone now, 'fore I have to knock some of ye down."

Then he'd run by that chest and beat on it, says, "He ain't in there. You all leave that chest alone. He's dead just like I told ye. Now you men march right on back to the King and tell him I done got shet of them giants and there ain't ary one left."

Well, Jack fin'ly made like he'd done run the army off. Let the old giant out the chest. He was just a-shakin', says, "Jack, I sure do thank ye for not lettin' all them men find out where I was at."

So Jack took the old giant on down to the depot, put him on a freight train, and they hauled him off to China.

The King paid Jack two thousand dollars for bakin' the old giant lady, but he said he couldn't allow him nothin' on the old giant be-cause the trade they'd made was that Jack had to bring in the heads.

Jack didn't care none about that, 'cause his overhall pockets were just a-bulgin' with money when he got back home. He didn't have to clear that newground for the King, neither. He paid his two brothers, Will and Tom, to do it for him.

And the last time I went down to see Jack he was a-doin' real well.

JACK AND THE BULL

One time Jack was bound out to a man who was rich and had lots of land and cattle. The old man liked Jack and treated him all right, but his old wife she didn't like Jack a bit, just hated him, and she treated him mean ever' chance she got. They had three girls at that house and they didn't like Jack much either. He had to work awful hard, and all he got for it was a few ragged clothes and scrappy vittles.

Then one day the old woman decided she'd try to get rid of Jack by starvin' him to death. She'd fix breakfast while Jack was gone to milk the cows of a mornin' and she'd fix supper when he milked of an evenin', and at dinner time she just wouldn't call Jack to come and eat at all.

So it wasn't long till Jack did get to starvin'. He got so weak he could hardly walk. And one evenin' when Jack was goin' up in the pasture to drive the cows down, he just couldn't make it; he gave plumb out and sat down on a rock. He didn't know what to do.

19

Then he saw a strange black bull come out of the woods; jumped over in the pasture and walked up to Jack, says, "What's the matter, Jack?"

Jack told him; then the bull says, "You're no need to worry about that any more, Jack. You just screw off my left horn and you'll find bread, and screw off my right horn and you'll find milk."

Jack took off the bull's left horn and gave it a shake and out fell as fine a little pone of bread as ever you'd want. Jack grabbed it up and started eatin'. Then Jack took off the right horn and when he tipped it up the milk just come a-pourin' out. It wouldn't empty no matter how long you tipped it. So Jack shook out some more pones of bread and held the milk horn in one hand drinkin' out of it like a cup and he eat all he wanted. Then he screwed the horns back on the bull and told him he sure was much obliged.

Well, the bull stayed there and Jack got fat as a pig. The old woman she wondered how Jack could be gainin' flesh when she wasn't givin' him anything to eat. She saw how the strange bull had taken up with Jack and she finally decided to find out where Jack was gettin' his rations.

Now one of their girls was one-eyed. The old woman sent her to spy on Jack and his bull. The girl got behind a bush, but Jack saw her. So he got out his fiddle and fiddled that one eye shut in no time. Eat his supper and the girl slept right on, didn't see a thing.

Next day the old woman sent her second girl. She had two eyes, and Jack fiddled a tune twice as long as he did before. Then when he knowed both her eyes were shut, he eat his supper; and when the girl woke up there was Jack and his bull just standin' around. So she went back and told her mother she didn't see a thing.

The old woman she was mad. She called her three-eyed girl the next evenin' and told her if she didn't find out where Jack was gettin' his supper she'd whip her. So the three-eyed girl went to watch. Jack got out his fiddle and played another sleepy tune, played it three times as long as he did before. Well, one of the girl's eyes went to sleep, then another one shut to, but she didn't want to get whipped so she kept poppin' her third eye open every time it started gettin' sleepy and fin'ly Jack thought it was shut and went and got his bread and milk, and the girl saw him do it, so she slipped out and ran back and told her mother.

Well, the next day, the old woman told 'em she wanted a bull's melt to eat and that Jack's bull would have to be killed so she could get his melt. The old man tried to get her to let him kill some other bull. No, she had to have the melt out of Jack's bull. No other melt would satisfy her. So the old man fin'ly went and told Jack.

Jack didn't know what to do then. And that evenin' when he went to do his feedin' and milkin', he was so worried he was just about to cry. His bull came over to him, says, "What's the matter this time, Jack?"

When Jack told him the bull studied awhile, then he said, "This is what we'll do, Jack: when they get fixed to kill me, I won't let nobody near me but the old woman. You agree to knock me in the head and I'll let the old woman get a hold on me, and when you go to strike me, you make a mis-lick and hit the old woman, and then you jump on my back and we'll run away."

So the next day they sent Jack to drive his bull down to the house to be killed. The bull came right along, acted peaceable enough, but when the old man undertook to get hold on him, the bull r'ared around and backed off; wouldn't let the old man come anywhere near him. Then the old woman came out. Jack was a-standin' there with a big pole axe in his hands.

"Sook buck," says the old lady. "Sook here! Sook buck! Stand still now."

She came over to him with the salt gourd in her hands and he stood still and let her get to petting him and feedin' him salt. Then she laid hold on his horns and hollered, "Run here quick, Jack! Knock him in the head."

Jack came a runnin', swung that pole axe, and when it came down it clipped that old woman right between the eyes, killed her dead.

Then Jack jumped on his bull's back and they lit out from there to seek their fortune.

They traveled on and traveled on and traveled on. Jack got his rations out the bull's horns and the bull eat grass beside the road and drank from the springs and creeks. Then one day the bull put his head down to drink out of a spring and a lot of blue blubbers came up in the water.

"That's a bad sign, Jack," says the bull.

Well, they went on a ways, and along late in the evenin' they heard another bull on ahead of 'em just a-bellowin'.

"I'll have to fight that bull, Jack. Don't you get scared, though. I expect I can lick him. You climb a tree when I start in to fightin' him."

Directly they came on that other bull, a big blue one, standin' in the road a-bellowin' and pawin' up the ground. Jack slipped off

his bull's back and cloomb a tree. The two bulls locked horns and went at it. They fought and they fought till fin'ly Jack's bull got the other'n down and broke his neck.

So Jack cloomb down again and unscrewed his bull's horns and eat his supper, and his bull picked grass by the road. Then Jack's bull laid down and Jack curled up right close to him and they both went on to sleep.

Next day Jack's bull started to drink from a spring and a lot of red blubbers came up in the water.

"Another bad-luck sign, Jack," he says. And then just about dark they heard another bull a-bellowin' up the road a piece.

"I'll have to fight again, Jack. I'm sort of tired out from that fight yesterday but I expect I can whip him. So don't get uneasy." Then Jack saw a great big red bull comin' down the road. The red bull stopped and bellowed and pawed the ground, and Jack cloomb a tree. The two bulls locked horns and just had it up and down the road, fought and fought and fought. Jack's bull got throwed a time or two, and Jack thought he'd get killed sure, but the black bull would get up again and fight right on. And fin'ly Jack's bull throwed the red 'un and kept him down till he gored him to death.

Then they eat their supper, Jack from his bull's horns and the bull from grass 'side the road, and after they'd eat, they laid down together and went to sleep.

Next mornin' Jack noticed his bull wasn't travelin' so fast as he had been, but they went on and went on, and then Jack's bull went to drink and a lot of white blubbers came up. The bull didn't say nothin'. He and Jack went on and went on, and just about sundown they heard a bull bellow up ahead of 'em, bellowed so loud it shook the ground. Jack's bull stopped, says, "I'm just about give out, Jack. I don't know whether I can lick that bull or not. Now if he was to kill me, Jack, you just skin a strop from the end of my tail to the tip of my nose and take off my horns with it. And if anybody was to bother ye, all you got to do is to take all that out and say,

> 'Tie, strop, tie!
> Beat, horns, beat!'

and they'll do any tyin' or beatin' you want done."

Jack said "All right"; and then they saw the other bull a-comin', big white one with his head down and swingin' from side to side. He stopped and pawed the dirt and put his head up high and bellowed again. Jack slipped off his bull and got up in a tree. Then the black bull put his head down and made for the big white 'un and they fought and fought and fought all over the ground, and Jack's bull put up an awful good fight, scratched that other bull up considerable, but he fin'ly got throwed and couldn't get up and the white bull killed him.

So after the other bull went off, Jack came down and did what his bull had told him about skinnin' that strop from his back and takin' the horns. Then he doubled that up under his arm and went on.

He traveled for two or three days, and then he saw he was gettin' right raggedy, and he decided he'd hunt some work so he could get him some clothes. First house he came to the next day he knocked on the door and an ugly old woman stuck her head out.

"What ye want?"

"I'm lookin' for work," Jack told her.

"Can ye herd sheep?"

"Yes'm, I know to herd sheep."

So the old woman hired Jack to tend her sheep, put him right to work. Jack got out on the mountain with the sheep, and directly a feller came through the pasture and got to talkin' to Jack, says, "You'll never see no peace with that old woman, Jack. She's a witch. You better watch out for her."

"Oh, I'll stand her off," says Jack. "I reckon I can handle her." And Jack looked to make sure his strop and his horns were there where he'd laid 'em down. That feller went off after a while, and pretty soon Jack saw the old woman comin' trompin' up the hill.

She stepped up to him, says, "What'll ye take, hard gripes or sharp shins?"

"Hard gripes," says Jack.

She grabbed Jack and went to chokin' him. Jack hollered,

"Tie, strop, tie!
Beat, horns, beat!"

And the strop unquiled and went after that old woman like a snake, wropped all around her and tied her good. Then the horns commenced gougin' her and butted her over, and she hollered, "Let me up, Jack, and I'll give ye a fine suit of clothes."

Jack told the horns and strop to quit and let the old woman up. She went hobblin' back down the mountain just a-cussin'. And when Jack went up in the loft that evenin' there was a fine suit of clothes hangin' in the rafters over his pile of straw. Jack laid down and slept good.

Next day here she came a-hoppin' up toward the pasture again.

"Which'll ye have, hard gripes or sharp shins?"

"Hard gripes, bedad!" says Jack.

The old woman came at him. Jack dodged her and hollered out,

"Tie, strop, tie!
Beat, horns, beat!"

And the strop tied her and the horns beat her till she says, "Let me up, Jack, and I'll give ye a poke full of gold and silver."

Jack let her up, and that evenin' there set a sack in the middle of the straw pile. Jack looked in it and it was full of twenty-dollar gold pieces and big silver dollars.

But next day the old woman came right back.

"Hard gripes or sharp shins?"

"Hard gripes," says Jack—

"Tie, strop, tie!
Beat, horns, beat!"

And the strop switched around that old witch-woman and the

horns knocked her down and beat her around first one way and then another all over that pasture. She kept on a-hollerin', but Jack let her have it that time.

"What I want," Jack told her, "is a fine horse and a good new saddle and a shiny bridle."

The old woman said Yes, she'd give him anything he wanted; so Jack fin'ly let her up. She went back down that hill just as hard as she could tear. And next mornin' Jack looked out and there was a pretty little mare standin' at the gate. So he put on his fine suit of clothes and tied that poke of money on behind the saddle and rode on off.

He rode on and rode on and eat at the cafes and stayed at hotels and directly his money was about to give out. And so one day he stopped by a farmhouse to see could he get some work.

The man hired Jack right off, says, "Yes, I'll hire ye. I need a boy to shake off apples for my hogs, and I want 'em watched, too. There's somethin' goin' with my hogs. I been a-losin' one ever' night here for about a week. If I don't find out what's gettin' 'em, I'll soon not have no hogs left."

So Jack shook off apples all day and kept a-watchin'. Eat his supper and went right on back; cloomb up in a tree and started in whistlin' and shakin' off apples. The hogs was all down there under Jack and next thing he knowed here came an old giant woman, went to feelin' under the hogs' bellies to see which'uns was fat; found two that was fat enough for her, picked 'em up and started on off with the pigs a-squealin' and a-kickin'.

Jack stopped whistlin' and hollered at her, "Hold on there, old lady! Where you goin' with our pigs? You wait there till I come down."

The old giant woman throwed down her hogs and grabbed up two big rocks, commenced grindin' 'em together.

"Oh yes, you little whiplin' devil!" she says. "If you come down from there, I'll grind ye to pieces in a minute." And she ground on them rocks till the sand just flew.

"Tie, strop, tie!
Beat, horns, beat!"

hollered Jack. That strop had the old giant lady tied hand and foot in half a minute, and the horns went to work on her and hooked her and beat her, and the pigs trompled her and bit her legs, and Jack got him a hickory and whipped her, and she hollered so loud that the farmer came runnin' up there to see what it was. He got the axe and chopped her head off. Then he thanked Jack and filled up his poke with money, and the next mornin' Jack rode on off again.

Jack decided to go home after that and save his money instead of spendin' it like he done before; and that's where he is right now, as far as I know.

JACK AND
THE BEAN TREE

Now this tale is about when Jack was a real teensy boy. He was a sort of puny young 'un then, and he was cryin' one day when his mother was a-sweepin' the house. She didn't pay him much mind, just went on sweepin' the floor. Happened she swept up a right big-sized bean, so she picked it up and gave it to Jack to hush him, get him out the way.

"Here, run plant this bean," she says. "It'll make ye a bean tree."

So Jack ran out and planted it, and didn't cry any more that day.

Next mornin' he went out real early to see how it was gettin' on, came runnin' back in, told his mother, "That bean tree's plumb through the ground and it's done growed up knee high!"

"Why, Jack!" says his mother. "Why, you little lyin' puppy!" And she slaps him.

Well, Jack he cried, but when his mother got the house cleaned up she looked out and saw it was like Jack said, and she felt sorry, so she gave him some bread and butter and brown sugar, and he hushed.

So the next mornin' Jack came and told his mother, "That bean tree's done got as high as a sure 'nough tree!"

"Now, Jack, you know you oughtn't to lie like that."

And she slapped him pretty keen. But when she happened to look out and see it, she came and gave Jack some ripe peaches and cream, and petted him a little till he hushed.

Well, the next mornin' Jack came a-runnin'.

"Oh, mother! My bean tree's done growed plumb out-a-sight! You can't see the top!"

"Now, Jack, you look-a-here! I just know that's not so. You surely must 'a lied this time."

And she slapped his jaws, real hard. But she looked out directly and saw it, so she went and got Jack, and gave him a big slice of cake and some sweet milk.

Well, nobody said anything about the bean tree for several days, till one day Jack said to his mother, "I'm a-goin' to climb up that bean tree of mine and see how high it goes."

His mother told him he oughtn't to do that, but seemed like he had his head so set on it she couldn't do nothin' with him. Jack said he'd pull her off a mess of beans on the way up and throw 'em down to her. So she fixed him up a little snack of dinner and he pulled out right on up the bean tree.

He kept on goin' — up and up and up. He cloomb all day, till it was way late in the evenin' 'fore he got to the top. Then, just about dark Jack came to a big pike-road up there. Went along it a little piece, came to a great big house, walked up and knocked on the door.

A very large woman came and opened it, looked down at Jack, says, "Law, stranger! What you a-doin' up here?"

"Why," says Jack, "because I wanted to come. This here's my bean tree. I just cloomb it to see what was up here."

"Well, you better get on back down again quick. My old man's a giant. He'll kill ye. He eats all the Englishmen he finds."

"Hit's a-gettin' late," says Jack, "and I can't get back very handy now. I don't know what I'll do."

"You come on in, then, and I'll hide ye tonight, but you better leave early in the mornin'."

So Jack went on in the house and the giant woman took him and put him in the bake-oven, set the lid over him. The old giant came in directly, looked around, says,

"Fee, faw, fumm!
I smell the blood of a English-mum.
Bein' he alive or bein' he dead,
I must have some!"

The old lady says, "No. You don't smell no English-mum. Must be that fresh mutton you brought in here yesterday."

The old giant looked around a little more, and fin'ly they eat supper and went on to bed.

When Jack heard the giant snorin', he came out the bake-oven and went lookin' around the house. Saw a rifle-gun a-hangin' over the fireboard, so he took that and went on back down the bean tree.

Jack played around with the rifle-gun a few days till he began to get sort-a tired of it, then he decided he'd go back up and see what else he could find. So he cloomb up the bean tree again.

The old lady was a-standin' out on the steps, says, "Why, you little scamp! Here you are back again. My old man'll kill you sure's the world. He saw his rifle-gun was gone. You better not try to come in here tonight."

"Well," says Jack, "you hide me this time and hit may be I'll not come back no more."

So she took him and hid him under the bread bowl. The old giant came in, says,

"FEE, FAW, FUMM!
I smell the blood of a English-mum.
Bein' he alive or bein' he dead,
For supper tonight I'll have me some."

"No. You must be mistaken," says his old lady. "Must be that mutton you killed the other day. That's what you smell."

The old giant started lookin' around, and she says to him, says, "You can look if ye want to. You'll not find none."

Fin'ly they eat supper and went on to bed.

When they were both of 'em fast asleep, Jack came out and looked around, saw a nice skinnin' knife. Decided he'd like that, so he took it and slipped back down the bean tree.

Jack's mother said that looked to her like stealin', but Jack said he figgered the bean tree was his'n and that ever'thing on it belonged to him.

Well, he played around with that knife a right smart while. Then he told his mother that he was goin' back up, but he said this 'uld be his last trip. Said there was just one thing more he wanted up there.

Now Jack took the hand-axe and cut the bean tree half through, left the axe a-layin' by the tree. Then he cloomb up to the giant's house again.

That old woman opened the door, says, "Why, buddy, what in the world you doin' up here again? My old man missed that knife, and he'll sure kill ye if he finds ye here."

"You better not speak too sharp," says Jack. "This here bean tree belongs to me, not to you." Says, "I reckon you'll just have to hide me again somewhere."

"Well," she says, "hit don't differ. Next time you come back I'm just goin' to tell him and let him kill ye. I'll not hide ye now, neither; unless you promise not to never come back here."

"I'll not promise," says Jack, "but if you hide me, hit'll be an accommodation."

Well, she took Jack and set him in a corner, turned the old giant's hat over him.

The old giant came in —

> *"FEE! FAW! FUMM!*
> *I smell the blood of a English-mum.*
> *Bein' he dead or bein' he alive,*
> *I'll grind his bones,*
> *To eat with my pones."*

"Just look, then," says the old lady, "and if you find him you can sure kill him."

So the old giant looked around and smelled around ever' place in the house tryin' to find Jack. Looked in the bake-oven and looked under all the bowls, says, "Sure seems like I can smell one, strong."

But he never did look under his hat, and pretty soon they went on to bed.

Then when Jack heard the giant a-snorin' right big, he came on out from under the hat.

Now, there was a coverlid on the old giant's bed, had little bells sewed all over it about a inch apart, and that was what Jack wanted so bad. But he knowed hit would rattle and wake the old giant up. So Jack went and fixed all the chairs up close to the bed, took the old giant's boots and hid 'em. Then Jack crope up and raised one corner of the rug. The bells went "dingle!" and woke the giant up, sat up right quick, hollered, "Scat there!"

Jack kept right still till the giant laid back down and set in to snorin' again. Then he went and eased the door open, went back and got him a good hold on the coverlid, jerked it off and made for the door as hard as he could tear. The bells rattled, "dingle! dingle! dingle!" The old giant jumped up, and started bustin' against all them chairs, a-hollerin', "Where's my boots? Where's my boots?"

Jack was just a-sailin' toward the bean tree.

The old giant kept knockin' them chairs around, says, "Where's my boots, old woman? Where's my boots?"

The old lady says to him, says, "They're right where you left 'em, I reckon."

Well, he had to get a light 'fore he found 'em. Fin'ly he got 'em on and lit out after Jack.

Jack was a-scootin' down that bean tree so fast you'd 'a thought he was fallin'. Got on the ground, he laid that coverlid to one side, grabbed up his hand-axe, chopped two or three licks and that bean tree fell down, down, down, clean across the fields and hills and hollers. Took it about an hour to fall all the way.

After the bean tree hit the ground, Jack went along it to see how far the old giant had got. Found him about a half mile off and he didn't have but one boot on.

Then Jack went on across the country to where the giant's house fell. The dishes were broke up pretty bad, but he and his mother got a lot of good house-plunder, all that wasn't smashed up when the house landed.

And the last time I was down there Jack was gettin' to be a right big boy, and he was doin' well.

JACK AND
THE ROBBERS

This here's another tale about Jack when he was still a small-like boy. He was about twelve, I reckon, and his daddy started tryin' to make him help with the work around the place. But Jack he didn't like workin' much. He would piddle around a little and then he'd go on back to the house, till one day his daddy whipped him. He just tanned Jack good. Jack didn't cry none, but he didn't like it a bit. So early the next mornin' he slipped off without tellin' his mother and struck out down the public road. Thought he'd go and try his fortune somewhere off from home. He got down the road a few miles and there was an old ox standin' in a field by a rail fence, a-bellowin' like it was troubled over somethin' —

"Um-m-muh!
Um-m-m — muh-h-h!"

"Hello!" says Jack. "What's the matter?"
"I'll just tell you," says the old ox. "I'm gettin' too old to plow

and I heard the men talkin' about how they'd have to kill me to-morrow and get shet of me."

"Come on down here to the gap," says Jack, "and you can slip off with me."

So the old ox followed the fence to where the gap was at and Jack let the bars down and the old ox got out in front of Jack, and they went on down the public road.

Jack and the ox traveled on, and pretty soon they came where there was an old donkey standin' with his head hangin' down over the gate, a-goin' —

> *"Wahn-n-n-eh!*
> *Wahn-n-n-eh!*
> *Wahn-n-n-eh!"*

"Hello," says Jack. "What's troublin' you?"

"Law me!" says the old donkey. "The boys took me out to haul in wood this mornin' and I'm gettin' so old and weak I couldn't do no good. I heard 'em say they were goin' to kill me tomorrow, get shet of me."

"Come on and go with us," says Jack.

So he let the old donkey out and they pulled on down the public road. The old donkey told Jack to get up on his back and ride.

They went on a piece, came to an old hound dog settin' in a man's yard. Hit would bark awhile and then howl awhile —

> *"A-woo! woo! woo!*
> *A-oo-oo-oo!"*

— sounded awful lonesome.

"Hello," says Jack. "What you a-howlin' so for?"

"Oh, law me!" says the old dog. "The boys took me coon-huntin' last night, cut a tree where the coon had got up in it. I got hold on the coon all right, but my teeth are all gone and hit

got loose from me. They said they were goin' to kill me today, get shet of me."

"Come on, go with us," says Jack.

So the old dog scrouged under the gate.

The old donkey says to him, "Get up on my back and ride, if you want to."

Jack holp the old dog up behind him, and they went on down the public road.

Came to a old tomcat climbin' along the fence. Hit was a-squallin' and meowin', stop ever' now and then, sit down on the top rail—

> *"Meow-ow!*
> *Meow-ow-ow!"*

—sounded right pitiful.

"Hello!" says Jack. "What's the matter you squallin' so?"

"Oh, law!" says the old cat. "I caught a rat out in the barn this mornin', but my teeth are gettin' so old and bad I let him go. I heard 'em talkin' about killin' me to get shet of me, 'cause I ain't no good to catch rats no more."

"Come on and go with us," says Jack.

So the old cat jumped down off the fence.

The old donkey says, "Hop up there on my back and you can ride."

The old cat jumped up, got behind the dog, and they went on down the public road.

Came to where they saw an old rooster settin' on a fence post, crowin' like it was midnight, makin' the awfulest lonesome racket—

"Ur rook-a-roo!
Ur-r-r rook-a-roo-oo-oo!"

"Hello!" says Jack. "What's troublin' you?"

"Law me!" says the old rooster. "Company's comin' today and I heard 'em say they were goin' to kill me, put me in a pie."

"Come on with us," says Jack.

Old rooster flew on down, got behind the cat, says, "All right, boys. Let's go!"

So they went right on down the highway. That was about all could get on the old donkey's back. The old rooster was right on top its tail and a-havin' a sort of hard time stayin' on. They traveled on, traveled on, till hit got plumb dark.

"Well," says Jack, "we got to get off the road and find us a place to stay tonight."

Directly they came to a little path leadin' off in the woods, decided to take that, see could they find 'em a stayin' place in there. Went on a right smart piece further, and 'way along up late in the night they came to a little house, didn't have no clearin' around it. Jack hollered hello at the fence, but there didn't nobody answer.

"Come on," says the old donkey. "Let's go in-vestigate that place."

Well, there wasn't nobody ever came to the door and there wasn't nobody around back of the house, so directly they went on in. Found a right smart lot of good somethin' to eat in there.

Jack says, "Now, who in the world do you reckon could be a-livin' out here in such a wilder-ness of a place as this?"

"Well," says the old donkey, "hit's my o-pinion that a gang of highway robbers lives out here."

So Jack says, "Then hit looks like to me we might as well take up and stay here. If they've done stole all these vittles, we got as much right to 'em as they have."

"Yes," says the old dog, "that's exactly what I think, too. But if we stay, I believe we better get fixed for a fight. I expect they'll be comin' back in here about midnight."

"That's just what I was goin' to say," says the old cat. "I bet it's pretty close to midnight right now."

"Hit lacks about a hour," says the old rooster.

"Come on, then," says Jack. "Let's all of us get set to fight 'em." The ox said he'd stay out in the yard. The old donkey said he'd take up his stand on the porch just outside the door. The dog said he'd get in behind the door and fight from there. The old tomcat got down in the fireplace, and the old rooster flew up on the comb of the roof, says, "If you boys need any help now, just call on me, call on me-e-e!"

They all waited awhile. Heard somebody comin' directly; hit was seven highway robbers. They came on till they got pretty close to the house, then they told one of 'em to go on in and start up a fire so's they could have a light to see to get in and so they could divide out the money they'd stole that day.

One man went on in the house, the other six waited outside the gate.

That man went to the fireplace, got down on his knees to blow

up the fire. The cat had his head right down on the hearth-rock and that man thought its eyes was coals of fire. Time he blowed in that old cat's eyes, it reached out its claws right quick and scratched him down both cheeks. The robber hollered and headed for the door. The dog ran out and bit him in the leg. He shook it off and ran on the porch and the old donkey raised up and kicked him on out in the yard. The ox caught him up on its horns and ran to the fence and threw him out in the bresh. About that time the old rooster settin' up there on top of the house started in to crowin' right big.

The other robbers, time they heard all that racket, they put out from there just as fast as they could run. The one they'd sent in the house finally got up and started runnin' like a streak, caught up with 'em in no time. They said to him, says, "What in the world was that in there?"

"Oh, I'm killed! I'm killed!" says the man. "I won't live over fifteen minutes!"

The others said, "Well, 'fore ye die, tell us what it was caused all that racket back yonder."

"Law me! That house is plumb full of men, and they've even got one on the roof. I went to blow up the fire and a man in the fireplace raked me all over the face with an awl. Started to run and a man behind the door took me in the leg with a butcher knife. Time I got out the door, a man out there hit me with a knot-maul, knocked me clean off the porch. A man standin' in the yard caught me on a pitchfork and threw me over the fence. And then that man up on the roof hollered out,

> 'Chunk him on up here!
> Chunk him on up here!'

Ain't no use in us goin' back there with all them men in the house. Let's leave here quick 'fore they come after us."

So them highway robbers ran for their life, and kept on runnin' till they were plumb out the country.

Jack and the ox and the old donkey and the dog and the cat and the rooster, they took possession of that house, and just had 'em a big time.

But the last time I was down that way, Jack had gone on back home to his folks. He was out in the yard a-cuttin' his mother a big pile of stovewood.

JACK AND THE NORTH WEST WIND

One time Jack and his folks lived in an old rickety house on top of a hill, and this time I'm tellin' you about, Jack and his mother were the only ones at home. Jack's daddy was off somewhere on the public works a-buildin' road, and Jack's two brothers, Will and Tom, they'd gone off to another settle-ment huntin' 'em a job of work.

Well, winter came and directly the weather got awful bad. It turned off real cold and set in to snowin' and then the North West Wind commenced to blow, and one day hit got to whistlin' in through the cracks of that old house, and Jack and his mother nearly froze.

Jack's mother told him he ought to get some boards and fix up the house a little. Jack studied awhile over that, and he recollected that Will had broke the hammer crackin' walnuts, and Tom had used up all the nails mendin' the fence, and that there wasn't any boards except a few old rotten pieces at the barn. So Jack told his

mother, No, said what he'd do, if it was him, he'd go and stop that North West Wind so it wouldn't blow.

His mother asked him how in the world he could do that, and Jack told her he'd go find the place where the wind came out, take his old hat and plug it right in the hole.

Jack's mother told him, says, "Why, Jack, you know that can't be done."

But Jack said that was the very thing he aimed to do — said he could try it anyhow.

So Jack spent pretty near all one day splittin' his mother a big cnough pile of firewood to do her till he got back. Then real early the next morning he got his old raggedy hat and pulled out.

He traveled on, traveled on, traveled on, till he got a right far ways from home, and just 'fore dark he met up with an old man with a long gray beard.

He was standin' there one side the road, and when Jack got up to him, seemed like he knowed Jack, says, "Hello, Jack! What you up to this cold winter day?"

"I've started out to stop that North West Wind," says Jack. "We're just about to freeze to death back home."

"Why, Jack, you can't stop the North West Wind."

"Oh, yes, I can!" says Jack. "I'll stop it all right—just as soon as I find the hole where it comes out at."

"That might be an awful long way off, Jack," says the old man. "You just better come on up and stay the night with me."

"Much obliged," says Jack, "but I reckon I better keep goin'. Just come and go with me."

"Why, I can't let you stay out on the road, Jack. There ain't another house between here and the state line. You come on home with me and we'll have us a snack to eat and talk this thing over 'fore ye go any further."

Well, Jack was pretty hungry, so he went on home with the old man, and they fixed up a good dinner, and Jack didn't have to be begged to sit down at the table. They got done eatin' directly and Jack helped get the dishes washed up. Then the old man says to Jack, says, "Now, Jack, you ought to go on back home tonight and look after your mother. If you do that, I'll give ye a nice present. I've got a tablecloth here and all you have to do is lay it out and say,

> 'Spread, tablecloth! Spread!'

and ever'thing'll come on it that anybody'd want to eat."

"All right," says Jack. "That would be a mighty nice thing to have. We ain't got much to eat just now, anyway."

So the old man wrapped up that tablecloth ready for Jack to start, says, "Now, Jack, you be sure and not stop at this next house back down the road. There's some awful rowdy boys live there, and if you hang around 'em much, they're liable to steal your tablecloth."

Well, Jack thanked the old man and took his tablecloth and went on.

He came to that house and those boys happened to be out in the yard. They came out in the road and started talkin' to Jack and Jack played with 'em awhile, and then they begged Jack to stop and lay up with 'em that night. It was gettin' 'way along late in the evenin', so Jack he went on in, and directly the boys got to askin' him why he had that tablecloth under his arm. Jack didn't tell 'em at first, but they got to pesterin' him and teasin' him so that finally Jack told 'em. They wouldn't believe him and started makin' fun of him till Jack unrolled it, said,

"Spread, tablecloth! Spread!"

And all manner of good vittles came out on it. So they all sat down and eat a big supper. Then Jack rolled it back up.

Well, that night after Jack was asleep, the boys took another tablecloth and put it in the place of Jack's. And the next morning Jack was up early and got back in home.

He came on in the house, his mother says, "Well, Jack, ye never stopped that Wind. Hit's a-blowin' right on."

"No," says Jack, "I never got to the place where it come out at. An old man gave me a present to come on back home."

"What did he give ye, Jack?"

So Jack told her about the tablecloth and what it could do.

"You try it out, then," his mother says. "I sure would like to see that."

Jack laid it out, says,

"Spread, tablecloth! Spread!"

But there didn't ever a thing come on it.

So Jack's mother took his tablecloth and cut it up. Made him a shirt out of it.

Jack stayed on at home about a week, and then that North West Wind got to blowin' hard again. So one day Jack told his mother, says, "I'm a-goin' to try again about stoppin' that wind, now, and you needn't look for me back till I get it stopped."

So Jack got his mother up a big pile of firewood and pulled out again. Took the same route he took before, and when he came to where that old man lived, Jack slipped through a field so he wouldn't be seen. Got back in the road and went on. He came to a mill after a while, and there was the old man just comin' out with his turn of meal on his shoulder, says, "Hello, Jack! Where you started to again this cold day?"

"I'm a-goin' to stop that North West Wind, uncle," says Jack, "and I'm goin' on this time till I get it plumb stopped."

"Why, you'll freeze to death 'fore ye get to where that Wind comes out, Jack. You better just turn around and come on back up to the house with me."

"I ain't goin' to fool with you," says Jack. "That old tablecloth you gave me wouldn't do what you said it would."

"Did you stop at that house where I told ye not to stop at?"

"Yes. I stayed the night there."

"They've got your tablecloth, Jack. You just go on home with me now, and I'll see if I haven't got somethin' else to give ye. We'll build us up a good warm fire and fix a little somethin' to eat too."

Well, Jack was gettin' pretty cold and he was hungry, so he went on up with the old man and they got dinner fixed. After they got through eating and got the dishes washed, the old man let Jack sit by his fire till he got good and warm, then he says to him, says, "Now, Jack, I'm goin' to give ye a rooster to take home and all you have to do is hold your hat under it and say,

'*Come, gold! Come!*'

and that rooster'll lay your hat full of golden eggs."

So Jack put the rooster under his arm and thanked the old man, and pulled out for home. The old man hollered after him, says, "You recollect now and not stop at that place where them devilish boys are."

Jack hollered back and said All right.

He went on and got past that house, but he met up with the boys in the road. First thing, they began to ask him what the old man gave him that time, and finally Jack had to tell 'em, and they said there couldn't no rooster lay eggs at all, let alone gold ones. Said Jack was makin' up a whopper. So Jack set the rooster down and took his hat, says,

"Come, gold! Come!"

and the gold just came a-pourin' out.

Then the boys said to him, says, "Why, Jack, you've just got to stay all night with us. You sure ought to show that trick to daddy when he comes in."

Well, they talked so good that finally Jack decided to stay. The boys' father took on a sight when they showed him about that rooster and he got Jack a box to keep it in that night. Jack slept hard and didn't wake up at all when the boys slipped in his room and took his rooster out of the box and put another one in the place of it. It was so near like the real one that Jack didn't notice it when he took it out the next morning and went on back in home.

When he got there, his mother said to him, says, "Well, Jack, I see you're back, and that Wind's a-blowin' right on."

"I never found the place where it comes out at, yet," says Jack. "Saw that old man again, and he hired me to come back."

"What did he give ye this time?"

Jack told her about his rooster, and she told him, says, "Let me see now whether it will or not."

Jack set the rooster out, says,

"Come, gold! Come!"

but there wasn't a single egg to come. The old rooster just jumped up on a chair and crowed right big.

"Hit's a failure, Jack. You made a bobble this time, too." So they killed the rooster and eat it for supper.

III

Jack stayed around home several days and tended to his feedin' and milkin' and kept up a good pile of wood by the fire; and then that North West Wind started blowin' the hardest yet. It blasted right on through the house and whistled around the chimney and it commenced snowin' in all over everything. Looked like a regular harricane was comin'. Blew through that old open house so hard it nearly put the fire out. Fin'ly Jack says to his mother, says, "I'm bound to go stop that Wind." Says, "And that old man ain't a-goin' to turn me back this time either. We'll freeze to death if that Wind ain't stopped."

Well, Jack worked hard gettin' up enough wood to do his mother a long time, and then he pulled out again. When he got near that old man's place, he cut out through the woods so he wouldn't see him at all.

But he hadn't gone any piece at all hardly 'fore he came on the old man out there a-rabbit huntin', says, "Hel-lo, Jack! What in the world you doin' back here again?"

"I'm goin' to stop that North West Wind," says Jack, "and I'm a-goin' on this time, too!"

"What did ye do with the rooster I give ye, Jack?"

"Hit wouldn't do a thing you said. We killed it and eat it."

"Did you stop at that house again, Jack?"

"Yes," says Jack. "I stayed the night there."

"They've got your rooster. That's what's happened sure." Says, "Now, Jack, you better just leave that North West Wind alone now and come on home with me again. We'll have to talk this over and see what we can do. No *Sir!* I'll not let you go no further this cold stormy day."

Well, Jack was pretty near give out with stumblin' through the snow, and he was cold and hungry too, so he let the old man have his way. They fixed up a good dinner, and Jack sat by the fire and got good and warm and rested, and directly the old man reached up over the fireboard and got down a little knotty-lookin' club, says, "If you go back this time, Jack, I'll give ye this club."

And he handed it to Jack, says, "Now, you can just take that club and say,

'*Playaway, club! Playaway!*'

and it'll do any knockin' you want done. Hit'll even knock up wood for ye." Says, "And this time I'm a-goin' to show ye it'll do what I tell ye, 'fore you leave."

So he took Jack outside the door and told Jack to tell it —

"*Playaway, club! Playaway!*
Knock up some wood!"

So Jack told it and hit went and knocked down a big tree, knocked it right down off the hill plumb into the yard, knocked it into firewood, and broke some of it up into kindlin'.

Jack just laughed and slapped his hands together, says, "I'll sure go home! That's the very thing I been a-wantin'!"

So he got the club, and told the old man he was much obliged and started on back home. The old man came out and hollered after him, says, "Now, you be sure and not stop at that house where them rowdy boys are."

"No. I'll sure not stop there this time."

Well, Jack got 'way on past that house this time and got on

down the road a piece and run up on all them boys comin' from the store.

"What'd ye get this time, Jack?"

Jack was so proud of this club he finally told 'em, and they begged him, said, "Oh, Jack! We got no wood in. If you'd just knock some in for us, we'll be awful much obliged."

So Jack went back with 'em and took out his club and told it to play away, and it went out on the hill, knocked down a big dead chestnut, knocked it right in the yard, and busted it every bit into firewood. All the boys just hollered when they saw that, said, "Just wait till father comes home now, Jack, and let him see what that club can do."

Well, they kept on after Jack to stay, till directly he said he'd wait a little while till their daddy came in. But Jack got very sleepy before that man came in and went off to sleep sittin' in his chair. And when the boys' father came home. Jack was a-sleepin' right on. They told him what kind of an outfit Jack had, and he says to 'em, says, "Hit's too dark now to knock up any more wood. Couldn't you boys try it out just a little on one of the big logs by the fireplace there?"

So the boys slipped the club out of Jack's hand real easy-like, and told it—

> *"Playaway, club! Playaway!*
> *Break one log there on the pile."*

The club started in on that log, banged away so loud it woke Jack up. Jack saw what was goin' on and jumped up and run out the door and hollered back,

> *"Playaway, club! Playaway!*
> *Knock down the whole house! Kill ever'body in it if they don't*
> *hand here my tablecloth and rooster, quick!"*

And 'fore they knew it that club had knocked out every log on one side of the house and had started in on the roof. The boys came a-runnin' with Jack's tablecloth and rooster, says, "Jack! Jack! Stop that club quick and not let it kill us!"

Jack got his club and picked up his tablecloth and rooster and pulled out for home right then, even if it was after night.

About daylight Jack landed in home, and when he got in the house, his mother says to him, says, "Jack, that Wind's a-blowin' right on."

Jack says, "Never you mind about that. We got all we'll ever need now. This here's the right tablecloth and it'll furnish us all we want to eat. And this here rooster'll give us all the gold we'd ever want to spend, so now we can buy some boards and nails and a new hammer handle and fix up the house against the North West Wind. And this here club'll keep in wood for us, all we want."

Jack's mother says to him, says, "I must see all that, Jack, before I know it's so."

So Jack took out his tablecloth and said,

"Spread, tablecloth! Spread!"

And he and his mother sat down and eat till they nearly busted. Then he got his rooster, says,

"Come, gold! Come!"

And there was his hat plumb full of gold eggs.
Then he held out his club, says,

"Playaway, club! Playaway!"

And the club went out on the hill back of the house just a-bangin' and a-knockin' till it had a big pile of firewood all broke up in no time.

Jack's mother watched it and nearly died laughin' at it. She says to him, says, "Well, Jack, you made out pretty well. We'll sure not be bothered about the North West Wind any more."

So Jack never did have to try to start out again to stop the cold Wind from blowin' in their house.

And he and his mother were both doin' pretty well, last time I saw 'em. They had that old rickety house fixed up tight against the Wind, too.

JACK AND
THE VARMINTS

Jack was a-goin' about over the country one time, happened he passed by a place where a man had been rivin' boards, saw a little thin piece and picked it up, started in to whittlin' on it. Jack was so lazy he never noticed much what he was doin' till he'd done made him a little paddle. He didn't know what he'd do with it, just carried it along. Directly he came to a muddy place in the road where a lot of little blue butterflies had lit down to drink. So Jack slipped up right close to 'em and came down with that paddle right in the middle of 'em — *splap!* Then he counted to see how many he'd killed.

Went on down the road, came to a blacksmith shop. He got the blacksmith to take some brads and make him a sign in big letters on his belt; buckled that around him and went on.

Pretty soon here came the King on his horse, says, "Hello, Jack."

"Howdy do, King."

"What's all that writin' you got around ye, Jack? Turn around so's I can read it."

The old King read it off:

"STRONG-MAN-JACK—
KILLED-SEVEN-AT-A-WHACK."

"You mean you've done killed seven at one lick, Jack? You must be gettin' to be an awful stout feller. I reckon you could do pretty nigh anything, couldn't ye?"

"Well," says Jack, "I don't know. I've pulled a few tricks."

King says, "Well, now, Jack, if you're up to that adver-tize-ment you got on your belt there, you're the very man I'm a-lookin' for. There's a big wild hog been tearin' around in my settle-ment, killin' lots of sheep. If you help us get shet of that hog, I'll pay ye a thousand dollars. All my men are scared of it."

"Well," says Jack, "I'll try."

So the King took Jack over on the mountain where that wild

hog was a-usin'. Time he got up in the holler a ways, he turned his horse around, says, "You go on up in the mountain and find it, Jack. I got im-portant business back home."

And the King gave his horse a lick and made it go back in a hurry.

Jack he knowed that if the King was so scared of that hog, it must be awful dangerous. Decided he'd just not get mixed up with such a varmint. Said he'd wait a little while and then he'd slip out and get away 'fore that old hog smelled him. Well, directly Jack got to plunderin' around in there tryin' to get out, heard that hog a-breakin' bresh up the mountain, and then he saw it comin'. So Jack lit out through the woods — him and the hog . . .

Whippety cut!
Whippety cut!
Whippety cut!

and the wild hog right in behind him.

Jack looked behind and saw it was gettin' closer; they say Jack com-menced jumpin' fifteen feet ever' step, but the old hog kept right on a-gainin'. Jack came out in a field, looked down it a ways and saw a old waste-house standin' there with no roof on it. Jack made for that house, ran in the door, and scrambled up the wall. That old hog was so close it grabbed hold on Jack's coat-tail, but Jack was a-goin' so fast it jerked his coat-tail plumb off. Jack got up on top of the wall, looked down at the hog standin' there with his forefeet up on the logs a-lookin' up after him. Then Jack jumped down and ran around outside, pushed the door to and propped it right quick with some timbers. Saw the hog couldn't get out, so then he pulled back to the King's house.

"Hello, Jack. Did ye do any good?"

"Why, no, King. I couldn't find no wild hog up there. Hunted all over that mountain, didn't see nothin'."

"Why Jack, that old hog just *makes* for ever'body goes up there. You must 'a seen it."

"Well, there wasn't nothin' but a little old boar shoat, came bristlin' up to me, kept follerin' me around. I ran it off a time or two, but it kept on taggin' after me. The blame thing got playful after a while, jumped up and jerked a piece out of my coat-tail. That made me a little mad, so I took it by the tail and ear and throwed it in a old waste-house up there, barred it in. I don't reckon that was what you wanted. You can go up and see if ye want to."

When the King rode up there and saw it was that wild hog, he like to beat his horse to death gettin' back. Blowed his horn and fifty or sixty men came runnin' up. They took a lot of Winchester rifles and went on up to that old house; but they were so scared they wouldn't go close enough to get a shoot at it. So fin'ly Jack he went on down there, poked around with a rifle and shot two or three times. That old hog went to tearin' around and when it fell it had tore that house plumb down.

So the King's men skinned it out. Hit made two wagonloads of meat.

The King paid Jack the thousand dollars, and Jack started to pull out for home.

The King called him, says, "I got another job for ye, Jack. They say there's a unicorn usin' back here on another mountain, doin' a sight of damage to people's livestock. Hit's a lot more danger-ous than that hog, but a brave feller like you oughtn't to have no trouble killin' it. I'll pay ye another thousand dollars, too."

Well, Jack tried to back out of it, but he saw he couldn't, so the King took him up there where they said the unicorn was, turned his horse around and just burnt the wind.

Jack watched the King out of sight, says, "Thousand dollars'll do me a right long while. I don't want to get mixed up with no

unicorn. I'll get out of here and go back another way. I'm not a-goin' to fool around here and get killed."

But Jack hadn't gone very far 'fore he heard that varmint breakin' bresh and a-comin' straight down the mountain. So Jack started runnin' around in amongst the trees as hard as he could tear. Looked around directly and saw that old unicorn so close to him it was just about to make a lunge and stick that horn right through the middle of his back. Jack reached out and grabbed hold on a white oak tree, swung around behind it. The unicorn swerved at him, hit that oak tree and stove its horn plumb through it. Horn came out the other side, and like to stuck Jack. Time he saw that, he snatched some nails out'n his overhall pocket, grabbed him up a rock right quick and wedged the horn in tight. Then he got him a switch and swarped the unicorn a few times to see could it break loose; saw it couldn't, so he pulled on back down to the King's house.

"What luck did ye have this time, Jack?"

"Why, King, I didn't see no unicorn."

"Now, that's a curious thing to me, Jack. Nobody else ever went in there but what that old unicorn came right for 'em. What did ye see, Jack?"

"Nothin' much, just some kind of a little old yearlin' bull, didn't have but one horn. Came down there actin' big, a-bawlin' and pawin' the ground. Got to follerin' me around pretty close and sort of gougin' at me with that horn, till fin'ly hit kind of aggravated me. So I took it by the tail and neck, stove its horn through a tree. I reckon it's still fastened up there where I left it at. We can all go on up and see it if ye want to."

So Jack took the King and his men with all them rifles up where the unicorn was. They wouldn't none of 'em get close enough to get a good aim, so Jack went on up to it, cut him a little branch and switched it two or three times, says, "See, men? There's not a bit of harm in him."

The men fin'ly shot it, and when it fell, they say it tore that oak tree plumb up by the roots.

Then they skinned it and brought back the hide.

The King paid Jack another thousand dollars, says, "Now, Jack, they've just brought in word here that a lion has come over the mountains from somewhere in Tennessee, been makin' raids on a settle-ment over the other end of this county, killin' ever'thing it comes across: cattle, and horses, and they say it's done killed several men tried to go after it. I told 'em about you, Jack, and they made me promise to send ye."

"Well, King, that sounds like the dangerest thing of all."

"I'll pay ye another thousand dollars, Jack."

"I don't know as I favor workin' any more right now, King. They'll be worried about me if I don't get back in home 'fore dark. Besides, my daddy's cuttin' tobacco and he needs me bad."

"Come on now, Jack. I'll pay ye two thousand dollars."

"Well, I don't know. I'll have to study on it awhile."

"Here's a thousand dollars down, right now, Jack, and I'll pay ye the other thousand when ye get it killed. I'd sure like to get shet of that lion."

"I reckon I'll do it then," says Jack — "try to."

So the King took Jack up behind him on his horse and they rode over to where they said the lion was last seen.

The King says, "Now, Jack, that lion's right up in yonder some-where. I'll not venture any further."

Jack slipped off the horse.

The King turned him around, says, "When hit smells ye, Jack, you'll sure hear from it!" And then the King left there a-gallopin'.

Well, Jack felt of that three thousand dollars he had down in his overhall pocket, said he'd try to get out of there for good and go on back home. But 'fore he'd hardly took a step or two, that old lion smelled him and com-menced roarin' up there in the woods, roared so hard it jarred the mountain. Then Jack saw it comin' — tearin' down trees, breakin' logs in two, bustin' rocks wide open — and Jack didn't waste no time tryin' to run. He made for the tree nearest to him and skinned up it like a squirrel. He didn't stop neither, till he was clean to the top.

The old lion growled around down there, smelled up the tree a time or two, and then it went right in to gnawin' on the tree-trunk. Jack looked, and it was a sight in the world how the bark and the splinters flew. It nearly shook Jack out the tree.

But it seemed like the lion got tired when he had the tree about half gnawed through; he quit, laid up against the foot of the tree and went sound asleep.

Jack waited awhile till his heart quit beatin' so fast, and then he 'lowed he might have a chance to slip down and get away from there 'fore the old lion woke up. So he started slidin' down the tree. He was keepin' such close watch on that lion's eyes to see would he wake up or not, Jack never noticed when he set his foot on a brickly snag. Put all his weight on that rotten limb, and hit broke, and Jack went scootin' down, landed right straddle the old lion's back.

Well, that lion started in roarin' and jumpin' around, but Jack he just held on. Then the old lion got to runnin' and he was so scared he didn't know he was headed right for town. Got on the public highway and kept right on till next thing Jack knowed they

were sailin' all around the courthouse. All the people were runnin' in the stores and climbin' trees gettin' out the way, and everybody shoutin' and hollerin', and the King's men came and started in tryin' to shoot the lion without hittin' Jack, till fin'ly one of 'em drawed a bead on the old lion's head and tumbled him up.

Jack picked himself up out the dirt, com-menced breshin' it off. Ever'body came over directly to see that lion, when they saw it was sure 'nough dead.

The King came along right soon and Jack says to him, says, "Look-a-here, King. I'm mad."

"Why, how come, Jack?"

"These men have done killed your lion."

"My lion? What ye mean, Jack?"

"Why, I'd 'a not had it killed for three thousand dollars, King. After I'd caught it and 'gun to get it gentled up, now, bedads, your men have done shot it. I was just a-ridin' it down here to get it broke in for you a ridey-horse."

So the old King went over to where his men were and raised a rumpus with 'em, says, "Why, I'd 'a felt big ridin' that lion around. Now you men will just have to raise Jack three thousand dollars for killin' our lion."

So Jack went on home after that; had a whole pile of money down in his old ragged overhall pocket.

And the last time I went down there Jack was still rich, and I don't think he's worked any yet.

BIG JACK

AND LITTLE JACK

One time there was another feller named Jack. He was a sort of big stout-like boy and they called him Big Jack. He had to get out and take work by the day wherever he could find it, but work got mighty hard to find down where he lived at. So he decided to go off somewhere else and hunt him up a job of work. Pulled out and traveled all day, and just 'fore dark he came to where a King lived at. Now this was another King, not the same one had all them giants and varmints to be killed.

So Big Jack asked the King for a job of work.

The King says, "Are ye a good hand to herd sheep?"

"Well, I don't know," says Big Jack, "but I'll do my best."

"Come on in, then. I guess I'll hire ye."

Big Jack came in the house.

The King says, "Now, I'll tell ye, I got a rule here with anybody I hire: the first one of us to get mad will get three strops cut out of his back, long enough to make shoestrings. Does that suit you all right?"

Big Jack said he reckoned it did.

Then the King says to him, "Well, your bed's ready now and you can just go on up."

Didn't say a word about Big Jack's supper. The old King went to eatin' and Big Jack went on to bed. He hadn't had a bite to eat all day and he was awful hungry.

Early next mornin' the King hollered up to him, says, "Hello! Come on out-a there! Your sheep's ready to go to pasture."

Big Jack came on down and started drivin' the sheep out. The King got by the gate and counted 'em. Never said a word about no breakfast.

Big Jack took the sheep on to pasture. Picked about all day and found him a few wild berries to keep from plumb starvin'. Drove the sheep in again about dark.

The old King opened the gate, counted 'em, says, "You're a pretty good sheep-herder, Jack. Ye never lost one."

Big Jack says, "Well, I done my best."

"Your bed's ready, Jack. You can just go on."

Didn't give him a bite of supper, and next mornin', hit was near daylight, the King hollered, "Hello! Get up! Get up! Come on here and take them sheep out."

The King counted his sheep and Jack stayed by 'em all day. He browsed around tryin' to find him some more berries, drove the sheep back that evenin'.

The old King counted his sheep, says, "You done just fine, Jack. You never lost nary sheep today." Says, "Go on now, your bed's ready."

Next mornin' way 'fore daylight, King hollered, says, "Hello! Get out of that bed! Come on! Come on! Get out-a there!"

So he counted his sheep and Big Jack took 'em on out. He was starved. Hunted ever'where to try and find him somethin' to eat, couldn't find a thing. Got back in with the sheep that night, he couldn't stand it no longer. So when the old King had counted his sheep, Big Jack says to him, says, "King, hit looks like I'm gettin' awful hungry. Ain't you goin' to give me nothin' to eat?"

"Why, no," says the King. "I never hired ye to eat; I hired ye to tend sheep."

The King looked at him, says, "Are ye mad?"

"Looks like a man ought to be mad," says Big Jack: "work for somebody all day and starve to death. That ain't no way to do!"

He stomped his foot and looked like he was about to cuss. So the King took hold on him and got him down: got out his knife and cut three strops right out of Big Jack's back.

Then Big Jack recollected about that rule and how he'd done agreed to it, so he hobbled on off and started down the road. Directly he met up with Little Jack — the same one that's in all them other tales.

Little Jack noticed him how he was limpin' along and asked him what was the matter. So Big Jack told him all about what had happened. Little Jack took him on to the doctor and got him fixed up. Told the doctor to take care of Big Jack, said he'd pay ever-what it cost when he came by that way again.

Then Little Jack, he went on down to the King's house to see would the King hire him.

The King says, "Ye ever herded sheep?"

"Why, yes," says Jack, "that's all I ever done at home — herd sheep."

So the King told him about his rule: first one to get mad gettin' three strops cut out of his back, and Jack says, "That's all right. I hardly ever get mad."

"Well, there's your room, Jack. Your bed's ready."

Jack went on up, but he didn't go to bed. He slipped out when they were all eatin' supper, looked through the keyhole in the kitchen door and watched where they put ever'thing after they got done. Then, when they'd all of 'em gone to sleep, Jack eased the kitchen door open, filled his pockets full of bread and got him some salt.

Next mornin' the King hollered him out, "Get out of there, Jack! Come on here and take them sheep out!"

Jack raised up and came right out. The old King drove his sheep through, counted 'em, and Jack took 'em on to pasture.

Sometime durin' that day Jack knocked a sheep in the head, skinned it out and built him up a fire. He roasted that meat, took out his bread and salt, and eat on it all day long.

That night the old King counted his sheep, says, "Hello here, Jack! One of my sheep's gone."

"Yes," says Jack, "I can't help that. A man's got to have somethin' to eat. I knocked one of your sheep in the head so's I could cook me some dinner."

"Well," says the King, "yonder's your bed."

Next day hit was the same thing. Jack killed him a right big sheep, just eat right on. That night the King noticed it. Jack went on to bed, after he'd slipped out and got him plenty of bread and salt from the kitchen.

Next day Jack killed him the biggest sheep in the gang. And that evenin' when the King counted his sheep, he says to Jack, "Hello now, Jack! You're goin' to break me up. I can't stand that no more."

"Are ye mad?" says Jack.

"Oh, no!" the King says, "I ain't mad, but I reckon I better not let ye tend my sheep no more. Are ye a good hand to plow?"

"Why, yes," says Jack. "Hit's a sight in the world how I can plow. My daddy says I'm the best hand to plow of any man in the country."

"Well, I got a lot of plowin' to do. I'll put you to plowin'."

Next day the old King went to the stable, holp Jack hitch up a big fine team of horses, put the plow on the sled and took Jack down to a big level field. The King held the plow up, told Jack to take it and showed him where to plow on that field.

Jack went to plowin', turned out good straight furrows till the

King left. And when the old King was out of sight, Jack let the horses drag the plow across the fields ever' which-a-way they were minded to. The team went to pickin' around at the grass in the field and Jack turned the ground wherever they picked at.

Got along the edge of the road directly, Jack saw a old man ridin' to mill on a little jenny, says, "Hello, stranger! Stop there a minute. What in the world is that you're a-ridin'? Law! I never did see such a trick as that before. Now, ain't that the prettiest thing!"

"I'm a poor man," the old man says. "You needn't to be a-makin' fun of my jenny. Hit's the best I can do."

"Makin' fun, nothin'! I'm not a-makin' fun. Law me! I want that thing. How much'll ye take for it?"

"Oh, no, you don't want this little old jenny."

"I do too now. How'll ye swap it for one of these here horses?"

"Why, I got nothin' to pay ye any boot."

"Boot? Why, bedad, I'd 'a 'lowed you'd want the difference. You swap me even for one of these horses, the trade's made right now."

So Jack took the harness off one of the horses. The old man turned the jenny in the field and rode the horse on off.

Jack got the little jenny 'side the other horse, put all that big harness on it, and started in plowin' again. Ever' time the horse pulled, the jenny would fly back against the plow. So fin'ly Jack took the swingletree, knocked the jenny in the head and killed it. Then he fastened it on behind the horse and com-menced drag-gin' it back'erds and for'erds across the field.

The King came along directly, ran out in the field, says, "Jack, what in the world are ye a-doin'?"

"Why," says Jack, "a man came along with this thing and I never saw nothin' as pretty in all my life. I thought you'd like it the best in the world, so I swapped one of your horses for it. Blame thing wouldn't plow, though, when I got it harnessed up, so I knocked it in the head with the swingletree. Now I'm a-draggin' it around to wear it out, get it out your way."

"Law me, Jack! You're goin' to break me up that-a-way."

"You ain't mad, are ye?" says Jack.

"No, I'm not particular mad," says the King. "Oh, I ain't a bit mad, but I don't reckon you need to plow any more today. How are ye about pickin' apples, Jack?"

"Oh, I'm a awful good hand to pick apples. That's mostly ever'thing I follered — pickin' off apples — at home and for all the neighbors. They say I'm hard to beat."

"All right," says the King. "You run down to the house and get that ladder settin' up 'side the barn. Get you a basket and a rope and go on up in the orchard, start pickin' off apples up there."

Jack went and got the ladder and basket and rope, and he got him an axe. Went up to the orchard and cut down three big apple trees. Set the ladder up sideways on one of the stumps and started pickin' off apples.

The old King wasn't very long comin' up there, says, "Jack! What in the nation you a-doin' now?"

"I'm a-doin' what you told me, pickin' off apples."

"What'd ye go and cut the trees down for?"

"How in the world you expect a man to pick off apples and them away up yonder like that? I always cut down the trees first. — You mad?"

"Why, no, I'm not mad at all; but you come here, Jack, and help me set that ladder up on one of them trees. I'll have to show ye how I want them apples picked off."

So Jack got hold on the ladder and holp him raise it up on a big high apple tree. The old King took the basket and rope, got up on the top round of the ladder and tied the basket up there. Jack saw him catch hold on a limb, jerked the ladder out from under him, left him a-hangin' up there in top of the tree.

"Hey, Jack! What made ye do that?"

"Well, now, King," says Jack, "you tell me what made you not give me no rations."

"You run to the house, Jack. Tell my old lady I said to hurry and fix you some dinner, quick as she can."

Jack ran to the King's old woman, says, "The King sent me down here; told me to kiss you."

"You confounded thing!" she says. "You get out of here or I'll knock you in the head with the broom."

Jack ran back out, bawled up to the King, says, "Hey, King! She says she won't do no such a thing!"

"You tell her if she don't I'll come down there and stomp her good!"

The old lady heard what the King said. Jack ran back and kissed her, and then went on in the kitchen and eat him a pile of dinner.

Jack took his time, and fin'ly walked on back up to the orchard, put the ladder up under the King and holp him to get back down. Then Jack got up the ladder and went to pickin' off apples.

The old King got back to the house, his old lady just lit in to him, says, "What in the world did you send that low-down thing in here to kiss me for?"

"Why, I never done it! *Did you let him kiss ye?*"

"Yes, I sure did! You hollered down here that if I didn't you'd stomp me."

The old King went back up to Jack and he was just a-r'arin', says, "Jack, what did you go and tell my wife that for?"

Jack came down the ladder about halfways, says, "You not mad, are ye?"

The old King says, "Yes, I'm mad! I'm good and mad!" and he made like he was comin' up after Jack.

Jack jumped down off the ladder right on top of him. They had it around awhile, till fin'ly Jack tumbled him, got him down, and cut three strops out of his back.

So Little Jack went on back to where he left Big Jack. Big Jack was all fixed up again, and Jack gave him them shoestrings he cut out the old King's back.

Then Big Jack went on home, and Little Jack paid the doctor and then he went home too, I reckon, 'cause the last time I saw Jack that's where he was.

SOP DOLL!

Said one time Jack started out to hunt him a job of work. He pulled out and traveled on till he got to another settle-ment, ran across a feller told him there was a man there wanted to hire some work done. So he told Jack where the man's house was at, and Jack went over there; stopped by the gate and hollered, "Hello!"

The man came out, asked Jack what did he want. So Jack told him.

The man told Jack to come on in; asked him what his name was. Says, "Well, Jack, I've got a mill on a watercourse down the road a piece, but I got no time to run it. I've hired several men to grind down there, but the very first night somethin' has always killed 'em. Looked like it was some kind of pizen. Now I thought I'd tell ye, Jack, so you'd know all about it 'fore ye took the job."

"Well," says Jack, "if you don't care, we might walk down there and look that mill over."

So they went on down to the mill. Hit was a old log house with a fireplace and ever'thing fixed for whoever tended the mill to cook and sleep down there. There were twelve little windows rather high-up on the walls, had no window lights in 'em.

Jack looked it over right good, says, "Bedad, I believe I might take the job."

The man says, "All right, Jack. I see you're no coward. Now I'll give ye half of what ye make and give ye your rations too. I'll go back to the house and get ye some meat and meal for your supper. And you can start in grindin' soon as anybody comes."

Well, when word got out that the mill was opened up again, lots of customers started comin' in and Jack had to grind right on till it was plumb dark.

Fin'ly got the last turn ground out and shut the mill down. He hadn't no more'n got the water turned out of the mill race when here came an old man on a sorry-lookin' mule, got off and walked in the mill with a little poke of corn on his shoulder. He had a long gray beard and he was one-eyed.

"Howdy do, Jack," he says. "How you gettin' on?"

"All right, I guess," says Jack. "I hope you're well."

"About like common," says the old man.

Then Jack looked at him, says, "I don't believe I ever saw you before."

"No," the old man told him, "I'm a stranger."

"Well, how in the world did you know my name?" Jack asked him.

"Oh, I knowed ye time I saw ye," the old man says. "I've come a long way today, Jack, and I wonder could you grind my corn for me. I couldn't get here no sooner."

"Why, sure," says Jack. "You wait here a minute and I'll go turn the water in again."

So Jack started the mill up and ground the stranger's corn for him; shut the mill down, and when he got back the old man says to him, says, "Jack, you're the first one ever done me right here at this mill and I'm goin' to give ye a present."

He reached in his big coat and took out a silver knife and handed it to Jack. Jack thanked him and the old man left. Then Jack built him up a fire in the fireplace and got out the skillet. Now Jack didn't have no lamp, but the fire gave out right much light, and it happened the moon was shinin' in all twelve of them windows. Made it pretty near as bright as day.

So Jack was cuttin' up his meat with that silver knife when all at once hit got thick dark in there. Jack looked up and there in ever' one of them little windows sat a big black cat. They all were a-lookin' right at Jack, their eyes just a-shinin'.

Well, Jack wasn't scared, much. He went on and put his meat in the skillet, set it on the fire and stooped down to turn it with his knife; paid no attention to them cats. But just about the time his meat 'gun to fry, Jack heared one cat light down on the floor. He went on cookin', and next thing he knowed, there was a big black cat a-settin' right up in the fireplace with him. Jack went to turn the meat over and that cat stuck out its paw toward the skillet, says, "Sop doll!"

Jack reached out right quick with his knife, says, "You better not sop your doll in my meat or I'll cut it off."

The old cat jerked its foot back and set there awhile. Them other cats stirred around a little; stayed on up in the windows.

Then Jack saw that big cat reach for his skillet again, says, "Sop, doll-ll!"

Jack come at it with his knife, says, "I done told you not to sop your doll in there. You try it one more time now, and I'll sure whack it off."

The old cat drawed back, set on there switchin' its tail. Them other cats stirred a little, one or two of 'em sort of meowled.

Then that cat sopped its foot right smack in Jack's gravy, says, "Sop! Doll-ll-ll!"

Jack came down with his knife right quick and cut the cat's paw plumb off. The old cat jumped for a window and all twelve of 'em went,

"Whar-r-r-r!"

and were gone from there 'fore Jack could turn to look.

Well, Jack went to throw that meat in the fire, and instead of a cat's paw hit was a woman's hand layin' there in the skillet, had a ring on one finger.

Jack took the hand out and wropped it in some paper, put it up on the fireboard. Then he washed and scoured his skillet, cooked him some more meat, and a pone of bread. Got done eatin' and went on to bed.

The next mornin' the man that owned the mill got up real early, says, "Old lady, you better get up and cook me some breakfast. I reckon I'll have to make arrange-ments about buryin' that boy today."

His old lady sort of scrouged around in the bed, said she was sick and couldn't get up. So the man fixed himself some breakfast and pulled on down to the mill.

There was Jack, just a-grindin' right on.

The man got in to where Jack was, hollered to him, says, "Well! I wasn't expectin' to see you alive, Jack. Thought I'd be buryin' you today."

Jack hollered back at him, says, "Well, hit's a good thing you don't have to do that."

The man hollered back in Jack's ear, says, "When you get that turn ground out, shut down the mill. I got to talk to ye, right now."

So directly Jack went and pulled the water-gate so's the mill racket 'uld stop and him and that man could talk.

Says, "Now, Jack, you tell me what happened last night."

Jack related to him about all them black cats and he told about the old man givin' him that silver knife.

The man says, "I see through the whole thing now. Hit's a witch gang. They wanted to have their lodge meetin's here in the mill. And when that cat sopped in the grease she pizened it someway or other."

Jack said he had an idea that was how it was. Said that was why he scoured the skillet. The man said hit was a good thing he done that. Then Jack told him about the cat's paw turnin' into a woman's hand, says, "You might not believe that, but I've got it right here to show ye."

Got that woman's hand and unwrapped it.

The man took it, looked it over, looked at the ring on it, says, "Now, I declare! Well, I'd 'a never thought it!" Says, "Now, Jack, you lock the mill up and come on back home with me. We got to tend to this right now. Hit's a good thing that knife was made out of silver. You can't hurt a witch with a knife, or a bullet even, unless it's silver."

So they went back to the house and the man's old woman was still in the bed. He asked her if she felt any better. She said No, said she'd not get up for a little while longer.

So the man says to her, says, "You want me to send for the doctor?"

She said No, said for him to send for some of the neighbor women. He asked her what women folks she wanted to come and she named out eleven women in the settle-ment. So the man sent word to 'em, and 'fore any of 'em got there he says to his wife, says, "Let me see your right hand."

The old woman sort of twisted around, poked out her left hand.

"No," says the old man, "hit's your right hand I want to see."

So she twisted and turned, poked out her left hand again. Then he reached over and pulled out her right arm and there wasn't no hand on it.

Well, the women folks came readily as soon as they got word.

The man says to Jack, says, "I been suspectin' my old woman was mixed up with that gang of witches, but I'd 'a never 'lowed she was the head of it."

Jack says, "Oh, surely not."

Man says, "Yes, I knowed hit was her hand time I saw the ring on it."

Well, when the last of them eleven women got in with his old lady, that man shut the door on 'em and fired the house. Them twelve witches started crackin' and poppin', and ever' one of 'em was burnt plumb up.

So Jack made a end of the witch gang in that settle-ment. And that man never did have no more trouble about his mill.

JACK AND
THE KING'S GIRL

Jack had an uncle lived a right smart distance from where he and his mother lived at, and he decided one time he'd like to go up and see his uncle.

Jack had done got so he wasn't lazy no more — not so much as he used to be. So he worked hard all week, gettin' in wood and fixin' ever'thing up around the place, then he pulled out.

Had to go right by the King's house on the way to his uncle's. The King had a awful pretty girl, but all her life she never had laughed, and the King had put out a adver-tize-ment that anybody that would make her laugh could marry her.

Jack got down close to where the King lived and that girl was out on the porch, she saw Jack, says, "Where ye started, Jack?"

Jack told her and she says to him, "I hope ye have a good time."

So Jack went on. His uncle was awful pleased to see him. They'd work a little and ever' night somebody'd come there to play and

make music. Jack had such a good time he plumb forgot about goin' back home.

So fin'ly his uncle says to him, "Jack, your mother'll be gettin' uneasy about you. She'll be needin' ye about gettin' up wood, too. Don't you reckon you better go on back home?"

Jack says, "Yes. I guess I had better go, pretty soon."

"You fix up and go back today, Jack, and I'll give ye a present. I'm goin' to give you a big darnin' needle. You can take that and learn how to sew your own overhalls when they get tore."

So he went and hunted up a big darnin' needle he had, put a long thread in it and gave it to Jack.

Jack pulled out, put the thread over his shoulder and let the needle swing down behind him.

Got down to the King's house; that girl was there, says, "You gettin' back, are ye, Jack?"

"Yes," says Jack. "Had a awful good time."

"What's that you got over your shoulder?"

"Hit's a big darnin' needle uncle gave me, to hire me to go back home."

"Needle?" she says. "Law me! I never did see a man tote a needle that-a-way. You ought to stick that in your shirt bosom."

"Well'm," says Jack.

Jack got in home, told his mother all about what a good time he'd had. Started in to workin' about the place, and he kept studyin' about gettin' back to his uncle's again.

So fin'ly Jack's mother says to him, says, "You've worked right good this week, Jack. You fix up your wood and all, and I'll let you go back to your uncle's again. But you mustn't stay so long this time."

Jack got ever'thing fixed up and pulled out.

Got to the King's house; that girl was there, says, "Hello, Jack. Where ye started this time?"

Jack told her. She says, "Hope ye have a good time, and get another good present."

Well, Jack and his uncle went several places that week, and Jack had such a good time a-hearin' fiddle music and banjo pickin' he never studied about goin' back home.

So one day his uncle says, "You better go on back home now, Jack. I'm goin' to give ye another premium. Hit's a swoard my grandpa gave me. Hit was used in the Revolutionary War."

He went and got the swoard and gave it to Jack. Jack started on home. He took that swoard and stuck it right through his shirt bosom and out the other side.

The King's girl was out in the yard, saw Jack comin', says, "Hello, Jack."

Then she saw that swoard stickin' out of Jack's shirt, says, "Law me, Jack! You've plumb ruined your shirt. Why, you ought to have carried that on your shoulder."

"Well'm," says Jack, "next time I will."

Jack got back home, played around with that swoard till fin'ly he got a little tired of it. So he worked right on all week, got ever'thing shaped up, says to his mother, "How about me goin' back to uncle's again?"

His mother let him go. Jack saw the King's girl out at the gate and stopped and talked to her awhile. Got back to his uncle's and had a big time. A gang of young folks 'uld come up there to Jack's uncle's place and they'd get to makin' music and singin' old songs, stay till nearly daylight. Then him and his uncle 'uld go some other place the next night, till fin'ly his uncle says, "Hit's about time you went back home, Jack."

"Yes, I reckon it is," says Jack.

"I'm goin' to give ye a nice present today. Maybe hit'll keep you home a month this time. I got a young colt here. You can take it home with ye and break it to ride. Hit'll take ye some time to get it broke good."

So he got a halter and brought Jack the colt. Jack thanked him and started on home. Got down close to the King's place, Jack got right down under the colt and got it up on his shoulder.

The King's girl saw him comin' a-totin' that colt, she ran out to the fence, says, "Law me, Jack. You the awfulest fool man I ever did see. You ought to ride that."

"Well'm," says Jack, "I'll try to think of that next time."

When Jack got home, he went to foolin' around with his colt, never thought a thing about goin' back to his uncle's till nearly about a month. Then his colt began to get sort of old to him, and he com-menced to talk about goin' back to see his uncle.

"Why, Jack," says his mother, "I 'lowed you wouldn't never leave your colt."

"Well," says Jack, "you can take care of it while I'm gone."

So Jack got all his work done up and pulled out again.

That girl was out in the yard and her and Jack talked awhile, then Jack went on to his uncle's.

They worked around the place a little, went huntin' a time or two, and ever' night some young folks 'uld come up there and Jack 'uld get to frolickin' with 'em. They made music and got to playin' Weevily Wheat and Skip to My Lou and runnin' eight-handed reels and all. Jack never did have such a good time and his uncle was an awful good hand to call figures. Jack plumb forgot all about that colt and his mother bein' likely to run out of firewood, till pretty soon his uncle said he reckoned Jack better be gettin' on back.

"Yes," says Jack, "I guess I ought to have went 'fore this time."

"I got a nice little heifer up here, Jack, and I'm goin' to give it to you so you can have a good milk cow to go with your horse. You keep it fed up real well, and your mother can milk it for ye."

Got him a line and tied that heifer by the horns, gave it to Jack. Jack thanked him and started leadin' his heifer on back home.

Jack got down close to the King's house, he saw that girl was out at the washin' place where they were all a-workin' with the clothes. So Jack remembered and he went to jump on that heifer's back; somehow or other he landed on it hind side to, grabbed hold on its tail and started in hollerin'. That young heifer started bawlin' and jumpin' from one side the road to the other, and went a-gallopin' on down to where the King's folks was a-washin' at. The King's girl looked up and saw Jack gettin' shook up and down and a-slippin' first one side, then the other'n, on the heifer's back and him a-hold of its tail and a-hollerin' for help, and she raised up and laughed so loud they heard her all over town. She stood there and laughed and slapped her hands till the King came out. And when he saw Jack and that calf, he started in to laughin' too, laughed till he had to sit down.

Fin'ly some of 'em caught the heifer and holp Jack off.

The old King took Jack over in town and bought him a new suit of clothes. Then he hitched up two fine horses to a buggy and rode Jack and his girl over to a big church and had 'em married.

The girl she went on home with Jack, and the last time I was down there they were all gettin' on right well.

FILL, BOWL! FILL!

This here tale's another'n about Jack goin' a-courtin'. And there's some more tales about Jack gettin' married; like that 'un about the doctor's girl, and there was that pretty girl down in Old Fire Dragaman's hole in the ground. 'Course Jack didn't marry all them girls at once. Hit might 'a been one way and hit might 'a been another. There's just different ways of tellin' it.

Well, this time it wasn't no King's girl. There was a farmer lived 'way back in the mountain had two awful pretty girls, and the boys were all crazy about 'em. This farmer, though, he was wealthy, and he didn't want the boys comin' around there, so he fixed up a way to get shet of 'em.

He put out a adver-tize-ment that any boy who wanted one of his girls would have to ketch 'em a wild rabbit and put it in a ring and make it stay there thirty minutes. That was his proposition: they would have to bring the rabbit and he'd make a ring ten foot across; then they'd put the rabbit in there and if it stayed thirty

89

minutes, they could have one of the girls. But if the rabbit failed
to stay that long, he'd kill the boy that had brought the rabbit.

Well, not many went to try, but some did, and the old man cut
their heads off. Directly it got so the boys mostly quit goin' down
here. That suited the old man fine. But then some boy would get
so struck on one of the girls, he'd venture, and get his head cut
off. Fin'ly it got so nobody'd go.

Well, Jack he got to studyin' about how he might get one of
them girls. His mother told him he better not do that, but Jack
said he'd just have to try. So he caught him a rabbit, and put him
a little snack of dinner in a poke, and then he got fixed up and
started out.

About twelve o'clock in the wilder-ness, Jack met up with an old
gray-bearded man. This old man looked like he was about a hundred years old, and he was walkin' with a walkin' stick.

Jack came along, the old man stopped, says, "Howdy do, Jack."

"Howdy do, daddy."

Jack looked at him, says, "I don't believe I know ye."

"No," says the old man. "I know you, though, and I know right
where you've started. You're a-fixin' to get killed, now, ain't ye?"

"I might, now," says Jack.

"Are you familiar with what you got to do to get one of them
girls?"

"Tol'able familiar," says Jack.

"Don't you think you'd just as well start on back home?"

"Oh, no," says Jack. "I'd never turn back. I'm a-goin' on down
there now."

"Well, I might help ye," says the old man, "if ye got any faith.
How's your faith, Jack?"

Jack said his faith was pretty good, says, "I'd sure be much
obliged was you to help me, daddy."

"Well, if you come down the road a piece with me, I'll test you
out a little and we'll see whether you got faith or no."

Got down the road a ways, the old man says, "Now, Jack, you take this stick here and go up there in the woods a ways till you come to a very flush spring. Then you take my stick and stir in that spring till the water turns to wine. And against ye get that done, I'll come up there with somethin' to help ye."

So Jack took that walkin' stick and went on to where there was a very bold spring comin' out the ground. Stuck that stick down in it and com-menced stirrin'.

Jack's faith was sort of weak when he started, but he 'lowed he'd have to keep on tryin'. He stirred right on, stirred right on, and pretty soon it looked like the water *was* turnin' just a little bit pink. So Jack's faith got stronger and stronger and the water got redder and redder.

Well, when that spring turned real red, there was that old man standin' there, says, "Well, Jack, you sure got faith. Now you get out your lunch and we'll eat a little and try some of that and see whether it tastes like wine or not."

So they did, and that water was just as good as any wine.

Then the old man says to Jack, says, "I've done made ye a drill here, Jack. You can take that and stick it down in the middle of the ring that man'll make and your rabbit'll stay in there till it dies; it don't differ how wild he is."

He gave Jack a drill shaved out of a stick. It was eight-square like a steel drill and about a foot long.

Jack thanked him and started on again.

Got down to that place where the girls were, Jack hollered the old man out and said he'd come to try for one of his girls.

The man told Jack to come around in the yard, and then he marked out a ring, says, "Now, you put your rabbit down in this ring and if it stays in there thirty minutes, you can take whichever girl you want. And if it don't stay in the ring thirty minutes, I'll kill you. You understand now, do ye?"

Jack said he did, made like he was goin' to turn his rabbit loose.

The man says to him, says, "I'll make ye another proposition; if you can make that rabbit stay in there thirty minutes, I'll just let you kill me and take all the money I got."

Jack went and stuck that drill down in the middle of the ring, and dumped the rabbit out the poke he had it in. The rabbit got up on its feet, saw that drill and took out around it hard as it could go, around and around and around.

The old man watched Jack's rabbit a-goin' around in there, and his eyes just stuck out. Walked around the other side the ring, watched it some more. That rabbit ran right on, 'round and 'round the drill. The old man kept takin' out his watch; fin'ly he turned around and went on back in the house.

So the oldest girl she went out, says to Jack, "What'll ye take for that drill, Jack?"

Jack says, "I don't know as I'd want to sell it right now."

"I'll give ye a thousand dollars for it."

"No," says Jack, "I'll not sell it."

So she went on back, told her daddy she couldn't make no trade.

Then he sent his youngest girl out.

She came up 'side of Jack, says, "Jack, I'd like awful well to buy that drill."

"Well," says Jack, "you can have it after thirty minutes is up."

"Aw, Jack," she says, "I want it now. I'll pay ye two thousand dollars for it."

"No," says Jack, "you wait till thirty minutes is out, and then we'll trade."

So she saw she couldn't do no good, went on back in the house.

Then the man said to his old lady, says, "You go."

She went out.

"Jack, I'd sure like to trade ye out of that drill. You can have one of the girls, right now; and I'll give ye three thousand dollars and ever'thing on the place."

"No," says Jack, "not till thirty minutes is out."

The old lady went on back, says, "I can't do a thing with him. He won't even talk about sellin'."

The old man looked at his watch, says, "Well, that thirty minutes is about up. I reckon I'll have to go on out and let Jack kill me."

Started out, picked up a big bowl off the table, and took that to Jack, says, "Jack, it looks like your rabbit's goin' to stay in there. You might as well kill me." Says, "'Fore you do, though, I wish you'd sing this bowl full of lies for me."

"All right," says Jack, "I'll try."

FILL, BOWL! FILL!
Recorded by John Powell at Marion, Virginia, August 1936.

Fill, Bowl! Fill!

Recorded by John Powell at Marion, Virginia, August, 1936.

Says, "Is it full?"

"No," says the old man, "only one drop."

> *"Oh, the youngest daughter she came out*
> *All for to buy my drill.*
> *I fooled around her, kissed her well.*
> *Fill, bowl! Fill!*

Is it full yet?"

"Just two drops, Jack."

> *"Oh, the old lady she came out*
> *All for to buy my drill*
> *I fooled around her, ki . . ."*

"Stop, Jack! Hit's full and runnin' over. Just cut my head off."

HARDY HARDHEAD

Now there was another King lived off 'way back in the country and his girl got witched somehow or other. So the King put out an oration that any man who could break the enchantment on his girl could marry her. Will and Tom heard about that and they decided to see could they do it. What they had to do was to go to the old witch that had put the enchant-ment on the girl and out-do her in every trick she put up to be done.

Well, Will was the oldest, so he went first. His mother fixed him up a cake and a bottle of wine, and early one mornin' Will pulled out. He traveled on and about twelve o'clock he came to a big oak tree and sat down under it to eat his dinner.

He took the cake and wine out of his poke, and just about the time he started in eatin' here came an old man with a long gray beard and a-leanin' on a walkin' stick.

"Hello, stranger."

"Hello," says Will.

"I'm hungry," says the old man. "Could you give me a little bite of something to eat?"

"No," says Will. "I ain't hardly got enough for myself."

So the old man went on off and Will eat his cake and drank up his wine and went on. He kept inquirin' about the old witch and fin'ly got to her house. He told her he'd come to try to break the enchant-ment on the King's girl, so she went and got out a big hackle. A hackle, that's a board about a foot square with a lot of long sharp iron spikes stickin' up out of it. Back in old times they used a hackle to comb the tow out of flax so you could spin it into linen thread.

Well, the old witch set that hackle on the ground and got up on a stump and turned a somerset, hit her back right on top of the hackle, and bounced off on her feet.

"Now," she says to Will, "you see can you do that. I'll lay a bet with ye that you can't do it."

Will put down what money he had and the old witch matched it, then he got up on the stump and when he came down on the hackle it stove into him and like to killed him. The old witch laughed and Will crawled on off and went back home.

Well, one day Tom decided he'd go. So his mother fixed him some cake and wine in a poke and Tom lit out. He got to that oak tree and started eatin' his dinner and here came the old man.

"Hello, stranger."

"Hello," says Tom. "What do you want?"

"I'm hungry," says the old man. "Could you spare me a little bite to eat?"

"Got no time to fool with ye," says Tom; "ain't hardly enough for me."

So the old man went off and Tom eat up all his cake and wine and hit the road again and fin'ly got to the old witch's house. She got out the hackle and made her bet with Tom, and she bounced off of it, and Tom lit on it and it stove into his back and crippled him up considerable. So he lost his money and had to hobble on back home the best way he could.

Then Jack he got to studyin' about it and one day he asked his mother could he go. She wouldn't let him, but he kept on beggin' her till fin'ly she said All right. She didn't fix Jack nothin' but an ash cake and a bottle of spring water.

Jack sat down under that oak tree and had just reached in his little poke for the ash cake when there stood that weezledy old man.

"Hello, Jack,"

"Why, howdy, daddy. Come sit down and let's eat a bite. It's not much, but you're welcome to half of it."

"Thank ye, son. How you gettin' on?"

"'Bout like common," Jack told him.

So the old man sat down against the tree, and when Jack took out his ash cake it was a great big spice cake instead, and when he got out his bottle of water it had turned into the finest reddest wine you ever saw. So he and the old man eat cake and drank wine and sat there a-talkin' about one thing and another.

Fin'ly the old man says, "Now, Jack, hit's been tried a right smart, goin' down there to break that enchant-ment. Ever' man that's been down there has lost money, and some of 'em have been killed on that hackle the old witch has got."

"Well," says Jack, "I 'lowed I might have some showin' maybe. Thought I'd go down and try it out, anyhow."

"Hit may be so I can help ye, Jack."

"I'd be much obliged if you would, daddy."

"Then you just sit right here till I get back, Jack, and I'll bring ye somethin' that might be a little use to you."

Jack waited and in just a few minutes the old man came back with a little trick made out of wood and all folded up.

He handed it to Jack and says, "Now, Jack, you can take this and lay it on the ground and unfold it and it'll make you a ship that'll sail dry land just like one of them boats they run on the ocean. If you got faith, all you've got to do is unfold that ship and get in it and say,

'Sail, ship! Sail!'

and it'll take you anywhere you've a mind to go."

Jack took the ship and thanked the old man. Then he set it on the ground and unfolded it and there was a great big ship.

Then the old man told him, says, "You take in every man you meet between here and the old witch's house. Call every man you see along the way. You may need a lot of help 'fore you can out-do that old woman. And here, you'll need some money too. Just take this poke with ye. It's got a thousand dollars in gold in it. You can pay me back when you get ready."

So Jack took the money and thanked him for that. Then he got in his ship and said,

"Sail, ship! Sail!"

and the ship went sailin' along right over the fields and trees and creeks and houses and fences just as pretty as anything you ever saw. Then Jack looked down below him and there was a man runnin' along buttin' his head against trees and stumps a-knockin' 'em every which-a-way. He'd run against a big rock, bust it up and go right along.

Jack hollered to him, "Hello, stranger! What's your name?"

"My name's Hardy Hardhead."

"Hardy Hardhead I think you are. Come on in my ship."

Hardy Hardhead got in the ship and they sailed on. Then Jack saw a man runnin' across a pasture-field eatin' cows up as fast as he came to 'em. Didn't take him no time at all to get one eat, horns, hoofs, hide and all.

"Hello, stranger! What's your name?"

"Eatwell's my name."

"Eatwell I think you are. Come on in here."

Eatwell got in and on they went. Saw a man directly runnin' along a creek bed drinkin' the creek up as fast as he went.

"Hello, stranger! What may your name be?"

"My name's Drinkwell."

"Drinkwell you are. Come on here with us."

Drinkwell got on board and they sailed right on. Then they saw a man run past their ship so fast it looked like he was flyin'. He wasn't runnin' on but one leg either. He'd hold the other'n up off the ground and still out-run the rabbits. Jack just did see him as he passed 'em.

"Hey, Runwell!"

Runwell didn't stop, but started runnin' circles around the ship.

"That's my name. What can I do for ye?"

"I'd like to have you in my ship," says Jack.

So Runwell ran in the ship and on they sailed.

Then they saw a man standin' with his head turned up like he was listenin'.

"Hello, stranger! What's your name?"

"My name's Harkwell. I can hear a chigger grittin' his teeth in a tall chinquapin tree over on that mountain yonder."

"Harkwell you must be. Come on in my ship."

Harkwell climbed in and they sailed on. Saw a man with his hand over his eyes like he was lookin' at somethin' 'way off.

"Hello, stranger! What can your name be?"

"Seewell's my name. I can see a gnat followin' that hawk a-flyin' around over there in England."

"Seewell I think you are. I'd like to have you in my ship."

Seewell got on board and on they went. Then they saw a man standin' on a hill with a long rifle raised up. He was a-sightin' over the gun-barrel a long way off somewhere.

"Hello, there! What's your name?"

"My name's Shootwell. Just wait a minute till I shoot the squirrel that's a-sittin' in that tree over there in Scotland. I'm goin' to hit him right in his left eye." *Bam!* "I got 'im."

"Shootwell you sure must be. Come on and go with us."

So Shootwell got in the ship and they sailed on to where the old witch lived. She came out and asked 'em what did they want.

"We've come to try out against some of your tricks," says Jack.

"All right," she says. "I'll bet ye a thousand dollars you've not got a man can bounce off my hackle and not get hurt."

"I'll take you up," says Jack.

"You got your money?"

"Here it is," Jack told her, and he counted it out.

Then she got out her hackle and got up on a stump, turned a somerset, lit on the hackle and bounced off, danced all around a-laughin'.

Then Jack says, "Hello, Hardy Hardhead."

"Right here, sir!"

"See can you do that."

Hardy Hardhead ran up on the stump and took a back somerset, came down head-first on the old witch's hackle, broke out ever' tooth in it and never got scratched.

"Well," she says, "you've got me beat on that. Now have you got anybody can out-eat me?"

"Eatwell!"

"Right here, sir!"

So the old witch brought out two big fat beef cattle and she took her stand by one and Eatwell got before the other one. Then she hollered, "Go!", and Eatwell jumped out and eat up his cow and a horse and a couple of sheep and some pigs, and the old witch hadn't even eat half of her cow.

So she says, "I'll bet you got nobody can out-drink me."

"Drinkwell!" says Jack.

"Here I am, sir!"

Well, that witch she took her stand at the head of one creek and Drinkwell went and got at the head of another one across the holler and Drinkwell had drunk his creek dry, two or three branches, and was a-drinkin' up the river 'fore the old woman had had a chance to take one swallow.

Jack had made a thousand dollars ever' time, but the old witch kept right on.

"Now the next proposition is to out-run me," she says. "Hit's seven hundred miles from here to the ocean. We'll take two eggshells and see who can get back first with his shell full of ocean water. Hit'll be salt water, so we can tell whether you run plumb there or not. And we'll bet another thousand dollars on this footrace."

"I'll have to raise it to four thousand," says Jack. So the old woman got the money and laid it down. Then she got the two eggshells.

Jack backed up to the ship.

"Runwell! Come on out here."

He gave him his eggshell and the old witch took hers and they got on the line. Jack hollered, "One, two, three — go!" And off they shot! They were out of sight 'fore you could turn around. Then Jack and the others sat down to wait.

Runwell got to the ocean and filled his eggshell full of ocean water, and started on back. He met the old witch about halfway. She knowed it wasn't any sense in her runnin' on, so she hollered to Runwell, "Hey! Wait a minute! Hit ain't no use runnin' ourselves to death. Let's sit down here and rest awhile."

Runwell stopped and they sat down and got to talkin'. Then she grabbed him and pulled him over, witched him sound asleep. She put an old horse's jaw-bone under his head. That jaw-bone was fixed so Runwell would sleep as long as the bone was under his head, it didn't differ how long. Then she mashed his eggshell and ran on toward the ocean. Runwell laid there hard and fast asleep.

Well, back there where the others were a-waitin', Jack began to get sort of uneasy about Runwell takin' so long. Then he saw Harkwell jerk his head up and listen.

"What do ye hear, Harkwell?"

"I hear somebody snorin'," he says.

Then Jack told Seewell, "Seewell, look well and see what you can see."

Seewell looked away off, says, "Runwell's a-layin' with his head on a jaw-bone, sound asleep. His eggshell is busted, and the old woman is pretty near the ocean. I think she's done witched Runwell with that thing under his head."

"Shootwell!" says Jack. "Shoot quick and see can you knock that jaw-bone out from under Runwell's head."

Shootwell raised up his old long-rifle and shot. Hit was over three hundred miles, but he hit it a dead center, knocked that jawbone thirty feet. Runwell sat up and sort of scratched his head. He looked around a little bit addled for a minute, then he saw what had happened 'cause there was his eggshell all busted up. So he jumped up, ran back to the old witch's henhouse, got him another eggshell, and ran on to the ocean. The old witch was stoopin' over to get up water in her shell, and Runwell gave her a good kick, knocked her clean out in the middle of the ocean-sea. Then he filled his eggshell up, and he was back in no time.

So Jack picked up all the money and he and the men got in the ship and sailed on home. Runwell and all the others went back to where they came from, and as far as I know they're all a-gettin' on all right.

I never did hear whether Jack married the King's girl or not, but anyhow she never was bothered with that enchant-ment any more after that. Jack went to where he met the old man and paid him back that thousand dollars in gold; and that ship, Jack's got it yet, I reckon. He's took me ridin' in it several times.

OLD FIRE DRAGAMAN

One time Jack and his two brothers, Will and Tom, were all of 'em a-layin' around home; weren't none of 'em doin' no good, so their daddy decided he'd set 'em to work. He had him a tract of land out in a wilder-ness of a place back up on the mountain. Told the boys they could go up there and work it. Said he'd give it to 'em. Hit was a right far ways from where anybody lived at, so they fixed 'em up a wagonload of rations and stuff for house-keepin' and pulled out.

There wasn't no house up there, so they cut poles and notched 'em up a shack. They had to go to work in a hurry to get out any crop and they set right in to clearin' 'em a newground. They decided one boy 'uld have to stay to the house till twelve and do the cookin'.

First day Tom and Jack left Will there. Will went to fixin' around and got dinner ready, went out and blowed the horn to call Tom and Jack, looked down the holler and there came a big old giant

106

steppin' right up the mountain. Had him a pipe about four foot long, and he had a long old blue beard that dragged on the ground.

When Will saw the old giant was headed right for the house, he ran and got behind the door, pulled it back on him and scrouged back against the wall a-shakin' like a leaf. The old giant came on to the house, reached in and throwed the cloth back off the dishes, eat ever'thing on the table in one bite and sopped the plates. Snatched him a chunk of fire and lit his pipe; the smoke came a-bilin' out. Then he wiped his mouth and went on back down the holler with that old pipe a-sendin' up smoke like a steam engine.

Tom and Jack came on in directly, says, "Why in the world ain't ye got us no dinner, Will?"

"Law me!" says Will. "If you'd 'a seen what I just seen you'd 'a not thought about no dinner. An old Fire Dragaman came up here, eat ever' bite on the table, and sopped the plates."

Tom and Jack laughed right smart at Will.

Will says, "You all needn't to laugh. Hit'll be your turn tomorrow, Tom."

So they fixed up what vittles they could and they all went back to work in the newground.

Next day Tom got dinner, went out and blowed the horn. There came Old Fire Dragaman —

"Law me!" says Tom. "Where'll I get?"

He ran and scrambled under the bed. Old Fire Dragaman came on up, eat ever'thing there was on the table, sopped the plates, and licked out all the pots. Lit his old pipe and pulled out down the holler, the black smoke a-rollin' like comin' out a chimley.

Hit was a sight to look at.

Will and Jack came in, says, "Where's our dinner, Tom?"

"Dinner, the nation! Old Fire Dragaman came back up here. Law me! Hit was the beatin'-est thing I ever seen!"

Will says, "Where was you at, Tom?"

"Well, I'll tell ye," says Tom; "I was down under the bed."

Jack laughed, and Will and Tom says, "You just wait about laughin', Jack. Hit'll be your time tomorrow."

Next day Will and Tom went to the newground. They got to laughin' about where Jack 'uld hide at when Old Fire Dragaman came.

Jack fixed up ever'thing for dinner, went out about twelve and blowed the horn. Looked down the wilder-ness, there was Old Fire Dragaman a-comin' up the hill with his hands folded behind him and a-lookin' around this way and that.

Jack went on back in the house, started puttin' stuff on the table. Never payed no attention to the old giant, just went right on a-fixin' dinner. Old Fire Dragaman came on up.

Jack was scoopin' up a mess of beans out the pot, says, "Why, hello, daddy."

"Howdy, son."

"Come on in, daddy. Get you a chair. Dinner's about ready; just stay and eat with us."

"No, I thank ye. I couldn't stay."

"Hit's on the table. Come on sit down."

"No. I just stopped to light my pipe."

"Come on, daddy. Let's eat."

"No, much obliged. I got no time."

Old Fire Dragaman reached in to get him a coal of fire, got the biggest chunk in the fireplace, stuck it down in his old pipe, and started on back. Jack took out and follered him with all that smoke a-bilin' out; watched where he went to, and saw him go down a big straight hole in the ground.

Will and Tom came on to the house, saw Jack was gone.

Will says, "I reckon that's the last of Jack. I'll bet ye a dollar Old Fire Dragaman's done took him off and eat him. Dinner's still on the table."

So they set down and went to eatin'. Jack came on in directly.

Will says, "Where'n the world ye been, Jack? We 'lowed Old Fire Dragaman had done eat ye up."

"I been watchin' where Old Fire Dragaman went to."

"How come dinner yet on the table?"

"I tried my best to get him to eat," says Jack. "He just lit his old pipe and went on back. I follered him, saw him go down in a big hole out yonder."

"You right sure ye ain't lyin', Jack?"

"Why, no," says Jack. "You boys come with me and you can see the place where he went in at. Let's us get a rope and basket so we can go in that hole and see what's down there."

So they got a big basket made out of splits, and gathered up a long rope they'd done made out of hickory bark, and Jack took 'em on down to Old Fire Dragaman's den.

"Will, you're the oldest," says Jack; "we'll let you go down first. If you see any danger, you shake the rope and we'll pull ye back up."

Will got in the basket, says, "You recollect now; whenever I shake that rope, you pull me out of here in a hurry."

So they let him down. Directly the rope shook, they jerked the basket back out, says, "What'd ye see, Will?"

"Saw a big house. Hit's like another world down there."

Then they slapped Tom in the basket and let him down; the rope shook, they hauled him up.

"What'd you see, Tom?"

"Saw a house and the barn."

Then they got Jack in the basket, and let him down. Jack got down on top of the house, let the basket slip down over the eaves and right on down in the yard. Jack got out, went and knocked on the door.

The prettiest girl Jack ever had seen came out. He started right in to courtin' her, says, "I'm goin' to get you out of here."

She says, "I got another sister in the next room yonder, prettier'n me. You get her out too."

So Jack went on in the next room. That second girl was a heap prettier'n the first, and Jack went to talkin' to her and was a-courtin' right on. Said he'd get her out of that place.

She says, "I got another sister in the next room, prettier'n me. Don't you want to get her out too?"

"Well, I didn't know they got any prettier'n you," says Jack, "but I'll go see."

So he went on in. Time Jack saw that 'un he knowed she was the prettiest girl ever lived, so he started in right off talkin' courtin' talk to her; plumb forgot about them other two.

That girl said to Jack, says, "Old Fire Dragaman'll be back here any minute now. Time he finds you here he'll start in spittin' balls of fire."

So she went and opened up an old chest, took out a big swoard and a little vial of ointment, says, "If one of them balls of fire hits ye, Jack, you rub on a little of this medicine right quick, and this here swoard is the only thing that will hurt Old Fire Dragaman. You watch out now, and kill him if ye can."

Well, the old giant came in the door directly, saw Jack, and commenced spittin' balls of fire all around in there, some of 'em big as pumpkins. Jack he went a-dodgin' around tryin' to get at the old giant with that swoard. Once in a while one of them fireballs 'uld glance him, but Jack rubbed on that ointment right quick and it didn't even make a blister. Fin'ly Jack got in close and clipped him with that swoard, took his head clean off.

Then Jack made that girl promise she'd marry him. So she took a red ribbon and got Jack to plat it in her hair. Then she gave Jack a wishin' ring. He put it on his finger and they went on out and got the other two girls.

They were awful pleased. They told Jack they were such little bits of children when the old giant catched 'em they barely could recollect when they first came down there.

Well, Jack put the first one in the basket and shook the rope. Will and Tom hauled her up, and when they saw her they commenced fightin' right off to see which one would marry her.

She told 'em, says, "I got another sister down there."

"Is she any prettier'n you?" says Will.

She says to him, "I ain't sayin'."

Will and Tom chunked the basket back down in a hurry. Jack put the next girl in, shook the rope. Time Will and Tom saw her, they both asked her to marry, and went to knockin' and beatin' one another over gettin' *her*.

She stopped 'em, says, "We got one more sister down there."

"Is she prettier'n you?" says Will.

She says to him, "You can see for yourself."

So they slammed the basket back down, jerked that last girl out. "Law me!" says Will. "This here's the one I'm a-goin' to marry." "Oh, no, you ain't!" Tom says. "You'll marry me, won't ye now?" "No," says the girl, "I've done promised to marry Jack."

"Blame Jack," says Will. "He can just stay in there." And he picked up the basket and rope, throwed 'em down the hole.

"There ain't nothin' much to eat down there," says the girl; "he'll starve to death."

"That's just what we want him to do," says Will, and they took them girls on back up to the house.

Well, Jack eat ever'thing he could find down there, but in about three days he saw the rations were runnin' awful low. He scrapped up ever' bit there was left and then he was plumb out of vittles; didn't know what he'd do.

In about a week Jack had com-menced to get awful poor. Happened he looked at his hand, turned that ring to see how much he'd fallen off, says, "I wish I was back home settin' in my mother's chimley corner smokin' my old chunky pipe."

And next thing, there he was.

Jack's mother asked him how come he wasn't up at the new-ground. Jack told her that was just exactly where he was started.

When Jack got up there, Will and Tom were still a-fightin' over that youngest girl. Jack came on in the house and saw she still had that red ribbon in her hair, and she came over to him, says, "Oh, Jack!"

So Jack got the youngest and Tom got the next 'un, and that throwed Will to take the oldest.

And last time I was down there they'd done built 'em three pole cabins and they were all doin' pretty well.

JACK AND
THE DOCTOR'S GIRL

N ow, there was a rich old doctor lived in the same settle-ment where Jack and his folks lived at, had an awful pretty girl. Jack got to goin' down there to see the girl and 'fore long she began to think a right smart of Jack. But the old doctor told Jack's daddy that Jack was too poor to be a-courtin' his girl. Said that 'fore any-body could marry her he'd have to be worth a thousand dollars.

Jack he studied about it a day or two. He was right bad struck on that girl. So fin'ly he decided there wasn't any chance of him makin' that much money there at home, thought he'd go off some-where else and hunt him up a job of work.

His mother fixed him up a sack of rations and he pulled out. Told his daddy he was goin' to earn that thousand dollars 'fore he came back.

So Jack went on, asked ever'body he met about a job of work, didn't find none. Traveled on, traveled on, got 'way out in a wilder-ness directly, didn't see no houses or nobody nowhere. Hit began

to get dark and he still didn't see no houses, not even clearin's. Went on and went on till it was a-gettin' 'way up late in the night, and then it set in to rain.

Well, fin'ly Jack looked out down a holler, saw a light away off. Struck out for where that light was at, came to a little log house settin' up 'side the mountain. Jack went and knocked on the door.

A little old bent-over lady came and opened it, says, "Law me, stranger! What in the world you a-doin' up here?"

"That's just what I'd like to know," says Jack. "I'm lost. I saw a light over here, so I came to try and find out where I was at."

"I can tell ye that all right. This here's a highway robbers' house, and they'll be comin' back any minute. If they find you here they'll kill ye sure."

"Well, I don't much care if they do," says Jack. "I'd just as soon get killed as stand out here and get drownded in this rain. I'm give out. I'd like mighty well to get to lay down and rest some."

"Oh, law! You can't come in here, stranger! Them highway robbers don't let nobody come here."

"Blame the robbers!" says Jack — "and you too! I'm a-comin' in there out-a this rain."

Jack went on in the house. There was a little pile of straw in one corner, so Jack got on that straw and laid down. He querled right up and went hard and fast asleep.

The highway robbers came in directly, had a lot of sacks where they'd been a-robbin' that evenin'. Opened the sacks and 'gun to divide the money. Then all at once Jack got to snorin' right big over there on his little straw pile.

One of them robbers jumped up, says, "What in the world is that racket?"

"Law, I forgot to tell ye!" says the old lady. "Hit ain't nothin' but a little old boy came here lost. I told him not to come in, but he came on in anyway, went back and laid down on that straw. He's plumb give out."

"Well, I guess we'd better kill him."

So one of 'em got out his gun.

The old lady says, "No, not kill him while he's asleep. Wake him up first. I never did like to see nobody killed in their sleep."

One of 'em shook Jack right good, says, "Wake up, stranger! What's your name?"

Jack sort-a roused up, says, "My name's Jack."

"Well, Jack, get up from there. We got to kill ye. That's our rules here. We don't want nobody messin' in our business."

"That's right," says another'n. "Dead men tells no tales."

"Well," says Jack, "you all can kill me if ye want. But I ain't got a thing except what clothes I got on. I got no money."

They looked him over right smart, got to feelin' kind of sorry for him, says, "Are ye a good hand to steal?"

"Don't know whe'er I'd be much good at stealin' or not. I reckon I could try. A man 'uld do anything to save his life."

"Well, tell ye what, Jack; there's a man back yonder got three fat oxen. He'll be drivin' one of 'em to town about daylight tomorrow. You steal that ox and we'll pay ye a pretty good price for it."

So, early that mornin' Jack started to go down to the road, happened he saw a stout piece of rope hangin' there on a peg, took it down and stuck it under his arm. Didn't know just what he'd do with it. Got down to the road, waited around tryin' to study out some way to steal that ox.

Heard that old farmer comin' directly drivin' his ox. Jack looked up the road and there was a sort of stoopin' tree there, had a limb went out right over the road. So Jack ran and cloomb up and got out on that limb, looped that rope under his arms and got it kind of covered up with his coat. Let himself hang down over the road. He got part of the rope around his neck, hung his head 'way over on one side.

The old farmer came a-whistlin' along directly, stopped, looked up at Jack, says, "I declare! Them highway robbers have done hung somebody! I bet there don't nobody know nothin' about it yet. Hit's a pity to let a man hang that-a-way. Might be somebody out of our settle-ment. I believe I'll just tie my ox here and run back yonder and tell 'em about it, so we can cut him down."

So he tied his ox and ran back to the settle-ment.

Here he came directly with a big gang of men, says, "This here's the place."

Looked up at that tree, says, "No, it ain't. Must be around the next turn."

And he led them men back and forth all mornin' a-lookin' for Jack and that ox.

Time Jack got back to the robbers they said to him, says, "Why, Jack, that's pretty good. Bein' as you done such a good job we'll pay ye three hundred dollars."

So they paid him, says, "About the same time tomorrow now,

he'll be back with another'n goin' to market to sell it. We'll pay ye to steal that 'un too."

Next mornin' Jack started out, didn't know what he'd do to steal that ox. Happened he saw a brand-new woman's shoe there on the floor where the robbers had dropped it. Picked that up and took it with him.

Jack waited down at the road. The farmer came along directly whistlin' and drivin' his ox. Jack ran out right quick and set that shoe down in the middle of the road, ran back and hid in the bresh.

The old farmer came up, saw the shoe, stooped over and picked it up, says, "Why, here's a brand-new woman's shoe. Believe it 'uld just about fit my wife. If I had the mate to it now, they'd last my old lady all winter. One shoe, though, that wouldn't do nobody no good."

Throwed the shoe back in the road and went on. Jack waited till he was around the turn in the road, ran out and got the shoe, took a near way through the woods and set that shoe in the road before the old farmer again.

He came along, looked down and saw the shoe, says, "Look-a-there! There's the mate to that shoe, and I've done gone and left the other'n back yonder in the road. Now, ain't I the fool!"

Picked it up, looked at it good, says, "Pair of shoes like that ought to be worth about three dollars. Why, I might sell 'em in town. Believe I'll hitch my ox right here and run back and get that other shoe. Hit won't take me but a minute. Saw, buck!"

Tied his ox and back he went to look for that other shoe. He ran about a mile 'fore he gave up tryin' to find it. Then he ran up and down that road all day tryin' to locate his ox.

Jack got back to the robbers' house, says, "Here's your ox."

"Why, Jack, you're the best hand to steal we ever saw. We'll pay ye three hundred dollars more."

Jack said he was glad to have it. Then they said to him, says,

"He's got one more ox, Jack, you steal it and we'll pay ye and turn ye loose."

"Well," says Jack, "I'll try."

Next mornin' Jack started out right early, didn't see nothin' at all to take down there with him. Got to the road and just sat there till he heard the old farmer a-comin'. Then he took out through the woods and up one side the mountain, started in breakin' and crackin' the bresh, and a-goin'

"Moo-oo! Moo-oo-oo!"

"I declare!" says the old farmer. "There's one of my oxen." Then Jack ran up another holler, broke bresh, went,

"Moo-oo! M-m-moo-oo!"

"And yonder's the other'n!" says the old farmer. "They must 'a broke loose, that's what it was. And I 'lowed somebody stole 'em."

Jack ran up in the head of a holler, broke bresh, and bawled like two oxen.

"There, now! There's both of 'em. I'll just have to tie this 'un here and go get 'em. I'll take all three to town and sell 'em all. Saw, buck! I'm goin' to tie you good."

So he tied his ox right fast to a saplin' and struck out through the woods.

"Soo-ook, buck! Sook! Sook! Sook!"

Jack he'd run up one side the holler, break bresh and just bawl. The old farmer 'uld run right after him.

"Soo-ook! Buck!"

Jack 'uld run down the other side, break bresh, and go,

"M-m-m-moo-oo!"

Well, Jack kept on runnin' and bawlin' till he got the old man all tangled up in a laurel thicket. Then Jack turned and gave him a dodge, went and got that last ox.

Got back up to the robbers' place, they said to him, says, "Jack, that's the beatin'est job of stealin' ever has been done in this country. We'll pay ye four hundred dollars this time and let you go."

II

So Jack put that thousand dollars in his overhall pocket and hit the road back home. Got in late that night. Next mornin' he told his daddy all about what he'd done, asked him would he go on up to the doctor's house and see about him gettin' that girl.

Jack's daddy went on up, says to the old doctor, says, "Well, Jack got in home last night."

"You say he did? Wasn't gone long. Must not 'a done much good."

"Brought back a thousand dollars."

"He did? Well, I declare!" says the old doctor.

"Yes," says Jack's daddy. "He wants to know when can he come up here and see that girl."

"Well, what I'd like to know," says the old doctor, "is how Jack got all that money."

Jack's daddy told him, and the doctor said that if Jack was such a good hand to steal, he'd have to try him out a little. Said for Jack to come down to his barn that night and see could he steal twelve horses out from under twelve men. Said that they'd be ridin' around in the barn lot.

Jack's daddy went on back and told him, says, "Jack, there ain't a bit of use in you goin' down to that old doctor's house no more. He says you got to come over to his barn lot tonight and steal twelve horses out from under twelve men, 'fore you can talk to his girl again."

Jack says, "Well, I'll have to try it."

So that night Jack went down to the doctor's barn, had a keg with him, started to open the gate.

One of them men a-ridin' around in there says, "Hello, Jack. Not come in here now. You just stay on the outside."

They saw the keg and thought Jack had him a plan to get 'em all drunk.

Jack went and cloomb up on the fence and sat there, watched 'em awhile. Hit was awful cold that night, and after a while Jack reached down and got the keg up, made like he was takin' a big dram out of it. Them men didn't say nothin'. Then directly Jack reached for the keg and tilted it up like he was takin' another swaller.

Fin'ly one of the men pulled his horse over to Jack, says, "Let me have just a little sup of that, Jack."

Jack handed him up the keg and that man took a little dreen on it.

Then another'n came over there.

"Hit's gettin' awful cold ridin' around in here, Jack. Let me have a small dram of that, will ye?"

Well, pretty soon they ever' one of 'em came over there and took a little taste of Jack's likker. They were careful to take just a little bit. They knowed it wasn't enough to make 'em drunk. But in about five minutes ever' one of them men drapped right over on their horses' necks, sound asleep. Jack had gone down to the drugstore and got a little chloryform to put in that likker.

So, when he saw they were all asleep, Jack pulled 'em off the horses and piled 'em all up in a stable trough. Drove the horses back to his house, put 'em in his daddy's barn.

III

Jack's daddy took the horses up to the doctor next mornin'; came back, told Jack, says, "Jack, you needn't fool with that girl any longer. The doctor says you got to come up there tonight and steal a rabbit out the pot, hit on the fire a-cookin', and him and his girl and his old woman all a-settin' there watchin' it."

Jack says, "Well, I can try."

That night the old doctor and his wife and his girl were all settin' in the house watchin' the rabbit and hit a-cookin' in a big pot on a old-fashioned fireplace.

Directly the girl looked out the door, says, "Oh, papa! There goes a big rabbit through the porch."

"You pay no attention to that rabbit. You watch the one in the pot."

So they set right on. Pretty soon the old lady says, "Law me! There's another'n! Why, hit's a heap bigger'n the one we got in the pot."

"You set back down now. Never you mind about them rabbits. You watch the one there on the fire."

Then Jack he crawled up close to the door and turned a great big rabbit loose right in the house. The old doctor jumped up out of his chair the first one, hollered, "Lordamercy! Look yonder what a big rabbit! Come on, you all, let's catch him!"

They all jumped up and started after that rabbit, ran it all through the house, under the table and under the chairs, till fin'ly they were all down on their knees a-pokin' around after it under the beds. It ran against the screen door directly, jumped out in the yard and got away.

They came back in to the fire; the old doctor says, "You better look at your rabbit, old lady, see does it need any more water."

The old woman went and raised the lid and there wasn't a thing in the pot but the gravy.

Old doctor says, "Blame Jack! I bet it was him got it."

IV

Next mornin' Jack's daddy brought the rabbit up there and showed it to the doctor. Came back directly, says, "Jack, I done told ye, you might as well quit tryin' to court that girl. Now the doctor says ye got to steal the sheet off the bed, tonight, and him and his old woman upstairs a-sleepin' on it. Said he'd have ever' window nailed down and ever' door locked tight, and said if you was to try to climb in at ar' window he'd shoot ye."

"Well," says Jack, "all I can do is try."

So that night the old doctor and his wife were a-layin' in the bed upstairs, heard somethin' rattle against the side of the house, looked over at the window, saw a head raise up and gouge against it.

"Hello, Jack! Ever-when you break ar' winder light out of there, I'll shoot ye sure. I got my pistol here."

The head jerked back down. Came up again directly, soused against the window, *Wham!*

"You look-a-here, Jack! I done told ye. You break just one light out of that window and I'll sure shoot. I mean what I say now."

The head jerked back down. Next thing it came up again, rammed right through that window, broke out ever' light in it. The old doctor raised up his gun, shot three shoots. They heard somethin' fall and hit the ground, made an awful racket; then ever'thing was real quiet.

Fin'ly the old lady says, "Oh, law me! You've done killed Jack!"

The old doctor listened to see could he hear Jack runnin' off, says, "I didn't go to kill him. I just wanted to scare him a little."

"Well, you've sure done killed him. I heard him hit the ground. Now what you goin' to do?"

"Well, I don't know."

"You better not let him lie there all night. Somebody'll find him, and the sheriff 'll come down here tomorrow, take you off to jail. Why, hit'll be first degree murder, and they'll hang you sure."

"Well," says the old doctor, "I reckon I better go down and drag him off somewhere and get him hid."

The old doctor got up and went on down. He was so scared he left ever' door standin' wide open.

His old woman thought she heard him come back in directly, holler up to her, "Old lady! Old lady!"

"What ye want now?"

"I got to have somethin' to wrop him up in. I might get the blood on me and that 'uld be a bad proof; it 'uld sure be known it was me done it."

"Well, there ain't a thing up here to wrop nothin' up in."

"Just get the handiest thing there is."

"I don't know what it 'uld be 'less'n I took the sheet off the bed."

"Well, get it quick and throw it on down here."

So she rolled up the sheet and throwed it down.

The old doctor came back up directly just a-laughin'.

The old woman says to him, says, "Now what in the world are ye a-laughin' at?"

"Why, that wasn't Jack. Hit wasn't nothin' but a old scarecrow he had fixed up, put his hat on it. He weighted it down with a big rock. That's what you heard strike the ground."

"Well, I'd like to know why you came back in here hollerin' for somethin' to wrop him up in. You tell me that."

"Why, I never hollered for nothin'!"

"You did, too. Now, where's my sheet!"

"What sheet?"

"My good sheet I throwed down to ye. What you done with it?"

"You throwed it down!" Says, "Law me! I bet five dollars I know where your sheet's at."

Next mornin' Jack's daddy brought the sheet back, says, "Here's your sheet, doctor. Jack says he'd like mighty well to get his girl now. Says he's got evidence you tried to shoot him last night. Got three bullet holes in his hat. Said he'd not go down and tell the law yet awhile."

"Oh, he can come on and get the girl now," says the old doctor. Says, "You tell Jack he needn't say nothin' to nobody about no shootin'."

So Jack married the girl and went to work. And as far as I know they're a-doin' well.

CAT 'N MOUSE!

One time the boys' daddy decided he'd give 'em a hundred dollars a-piece and let 'em go out by themselves to see what would they do with it. Told 'em to be gone one year and then to come back so he could see which one of 'em made the best out of his money.

Well, the three of 'em set out together down the big road. Then Will says, "Now, when we come to where the road forks three ways, we'll separate. There ain't no use in us goin' all together."

So when they came to a crossroad, they stopped and talked awhile, and directly Will called Tom off to one side and they went to whisperin', then they both came over to Jack and threw him down and took every cent of his money, divided it, and left Jack a-layin' there. Will took one side-road and Tom took the other'n. Jack got his senses back pretty soon and set there a little while tryin' to study what to do. Then he decided he'd go on and see what luck he might have, so he walked out in the middle of the crossroads and throwed his hat up in the air. Whichever road it landed in, he was goin' to go that way. Well, his hat landed in the road straight ahead, so he took it and on he went.

Hit was an old road, not traveled much, and pretty soon Jack landed 'way out in a lonesome wilder-ness of a place. Went on, went on; the road pretty nearly covered up with grass and briars, and directly he came to a fine-lookin' white house out there. Jack could see signs of somebody livin' there and he had to have some place to stay the night. He hated to holler 'cause he was so ragged and dirty, but he 'lowed there wasn't nothin' like tryin', so he hollered hello and waited awhile. Nobody came out, so he went to the door and pulled the doorbell. The door opened and a big cat came out. Jack didn't know what to think of that. The cat sat there lookin' at him and there didn't no person come to the door, so Jack hollered again, "Who keeps house?"

"Cat 'n the mouse," says the cat.

"Law me!" says Jack. "I've done got to a country where cats can talk."

"Yes," the cat told him, "there's an old witch out here. She got all my family but me and my sister. She witched her into a cat, then to a mouse, and me into a cat. She'll try to witch me into a mouse tonight."

Then Jack looked and saw a mouse creep out one side the door, says, "Well, is there anything I can do to keep the old witch from botherin' ye?"

"Probably might be," says the cat. "You can help me, but my sister, she'll stay a mouse. There can't nothin' be done for ye, once she gets you into a mouse. You stay here by the door tonight and kill any kind of big varmints you see and it'll keep the witch off."

Well, Jack got him a big club and got before the door, and when it got plumb thick dark all sorts of bears and painters and big wild animals came up the steps and Jack 'uld knock 'em and beat 'em with his club, kept on fightin' all night. Next mornin' that cat came out and it was a little bigger, looked a little bit like a girl.

"Now tonight," she says, "the old witch'll send middle-size varmints. You see can you keep them off, too."

Jack picked around that day and got what berries and such he could find to eat, cut him a middle-size club and when it commenced gettin' dark he got by the door again. Then all kinds of pizen snakes and wildcats and weasels and boomers and ground hogs came and tried to get in. Jack hit at 'em with his club and knocked 'em off the porch and kept on a-givin' it to 'em till daylight. Then the door opened and that girl came out. She was pretty near the right size that time, but she still had some signs of a cat's claws and whiskers and ears.

She says to Jack, "You done fine last night, Jack. Now tonight she'll send all sorts of little varmints. You'll have a time of it, I expect."

So Jack eat a few blackberries and huckleberries that day and whittled him out some paddles and swatters and took up his stand by the door when night came; and all sorts of pizen scorpions and insects and spiders and hornets and big ants came up and tried to cross the door sill, but Jack went to work with his swatters and his paddles and it was a sight in the world how he went after 'em. He thought there'd be a pile of dead things there when it got daylight, but when it got light enough for him to see, there wasn't a thing there on the porch.

Then the door opened and there stood the prettiest girl you ever looked at.

"You did real well, Jack," she says. "You come on in the house now and I'll fix ye somethin' to eat."

She baked Jack some cornbread and fixed him some coffee, and while he was eatin', she says to him, "Now, you won't have nothin' to contend with tonight but the old witch herself. You got shet of all the plagues she had. Now, when she comes in you be sure and not let her do anything in the world for ye. I'll hide, and you and the old witch can go to it. You remember now, if you let her do one thing for ye, she'll witch us both into cats."

So that night that girl went and hid somewhere, and Jack he found him a needle and some thread, pulled up 'fore the fire and went to patchin' his old raggedy coat. It wasn't long till a little ugly old wrinkled-up woman came hobblin' in the door, looked like she was about a hundred years old. Her nose and her chin was so long they hung down a-wobblin'. She got a chair and pulled up close to Jack, says, "Howdy do, Jack."

"Howdy do, ma'm."

"Let me do that for ye, Jack. It looks so awkward seein' a man try to patch."

"No," says Jack, "I'll do my own patchin'."

The old witch looked sort of out-done, but Jack kept right on, and directly he got up to fix him a little supper. Got some meal and a pan and started mixin' bread.

"Let me do that for ye, Jack. I never did like to see a man try to make bread."

"No," says Jack, "I can fix bread all right."

Then he went to the fire, raked him out some coals and set the skillet over 'em. Then he cut some meat and started it to fryin'.

"Let me 'tend the meat for ye, Jack. I never saw anything so awkward as a man tryin' to cook."

"No, thank you, ma'm," says Jack, "I don't want you messin' with my meat. I'll 'tend it myself."

Well, when Jack turned around to get his bread that old witch got hold of the knife and went to turn Jack's meat over. There was an old flesh fork a-hangin' there, big old fork they used to cook meat on. Jack grabbed that up and ran at the old woman with it, hooked her and rammed her right on in the fire. He held her down between the backlog and the forestick and such a crackin' and a poppin' and a fryin' and a singein' you never heard. Jack kept her there till she burnt up.

Then there stood that girl just a-laughin', says, "You sure got her then, Jack. There'll not be no more witchery done around here."

So she fixed Jack a nice supper and the next mornin' when they went out that place was just full of fine livestock—chickens and hogs and sheep and cattle and horses—and the road was cleared out and the crops all standin' in the fields.

That girl says to Jack, "Ever'thing here belongs to you now, Jack, for killin' that witch."

"You too?" says Jack.

"Well," she says, "yes; if you say so."

"I'll sure say so," says Jack; "you're the main part of the property."

So they went and got two fine horses and hitched 'em up to the surrey, and went to the store and got Jack a new suit of clothes and then found 'em a preacher and got married. Jack he went to work about the place 'tendin' to his crops and his livestock, and that young woman she cooked and did the washin' and the milkin' and churnin' and all; and then Jack got to studyin' how the year was about up. So he told the girl about how he and Will and Tom had started out, and said they'd better fix up pretty soon to go back and see his daddy.

So they got ready and pulled out with the team and buggy one mornin'. Jack had got his old clothes and throwed 'em in under the seat. That girl had a pet fox and they took it along too.

They came in sight of Jack's house and he said to her, "You wait here a minute. I want to see what all's done happened while I been gone, see if Will and Tom got back yet."

Then he put on his raggedy old clothes, put that fox under his arm and went on to the house.

His father saw him comin' and came out to the gate, says, "Hello, Jack. Glad to see ye. You look like you must not 'a had any luck; I see you got the same suit of clothes."

"Will and Tom come?" Jack asked him.

"Yes, they got in early this mornin'. They got new clothes and both of 'em married nice-lookin' women. You wait here, Jack, and let me go get you one of my suits of clothes so you'll have somethin' better to wear when you come in."

"No," Jack told him, "I'll just go ahead like I am."

So he went in the house, and when Will and Tom saw him in his same ragged overhalls and coat, they com-menced laughin' and makin' fun of him; and their wives they slipped around and pinned dishrags to his coat-tails. Jack didn't pay no mind. He talked to his daddy and his mother awhile. Ever' now and then he'd squeeze down on that fox and it 'uld say,

"Gold enough
But none for you."

Will and Tom they couldn't understand that. Then directly Jack went on back where he'd left his wife. He got his good new suit of clothes on again and then him and his wife drove the surrey on down to the gate. Hitched the horse and Jack took the pet fox under his arm.

Will looked out and saw 'em, says, "Who's that?"

Tom came and looked. "Ain't nobody we know. It's rich folks. What you reckon they want?"

Their wives, they came and peeked around the door. And about that time Jack's mother looked out the window, says, "That's Jack."

"No!" says Will. "Why, that can't be Jack."

"Yes, it is, too," says Tom. "It is Jack, and look what a pretty fine-dressed woman he's got."

"Law me!" says Will's wife, "hit'll not do for her to see the way I am." And she ran and hid under the bed.

Then Tom gave his wife a shove, says, "You run hide some-where quick. Don't let her see you in that old cotton dress." And she jumped off the porch and crawled in under the house.

Jack brought his wife on in and made her known to his daddy and his mother, and Will and Tom just stood around.

Fin'ly Jack's wife said to 'em, "I thought Jack told me you boys was married. Where's your wives at?"

"Mine's under the bed," says Will. "She can come out if she wants to."

She crawled out from under the bed, had feathers and dust in her hair. Then Jack's woman asked if the other'n was home, and

Tom's wife she scrambled out from under the floor with her hair full of trash and dirt all over her. Jack's wife spoke nice to 'em, and they all talked on awhile. Jack squeezed down on that fox directly and it said,

> *"Gold enough*
> *But none for you."*

And by that time Will and Tom knowed what it meant.

Well, Jack took his daddy and his mother on back with him and his wife, and they was all independent rich. Will and Tom never did do much good. And Jack and his wife and his folks they lived happy.

JACK

AND KING MAROCK

One time Jack met up with a stranger said his name was King Marock. King Marock was a roguish kind of feller, liked to play cards, and he was some kind of a witch too, but Jack didn't know that. Jack and King Marock got to talkin', and directly the King bantered Jack for a game of cards. So they started in playin', and Jack got beat seven times, but he had a little money left and kept right on, and then he turned it on King Marock and beat him six times straight, cleaned the old King out of every cent he had. So King Marock told Jack he'd play one more hand and bet Jack's choice of his three girls against the whole pile. Jack said All right, and he won again. But time he laid his cards down, King Marock was gone, and Jack couldn't tell which-a-way he went nor nothin'.

So Jack went to huntin' and inquirin' for King Marock. Couldn't nobody tell him a thing about where the King's house was.

Then Jack met up with Old Man Freezewell, and Jack asked him, "Do you know where King Marock lives at?"

"No," Freezewell told him, "but I'll do ever'thing I can to help ye find him."

Freezewell went and froze ever'thing over real hard that night. Next mornin' he came to Jack, says, "I couldn't find the King, Jack, but I found an old man knows where his girls wash at. Now, this old man keeps beer, and I've frozen all his beer up, and he's mad, but you take this here little rod and go ask him for a drink of beer. He'll tell ye it's all froze, and then you thaw it for him, and that'll please him, and he'll tell ye where King Marock's girls' washin' place is at."

Freezewell told Jack where that old man's house was located, and Jack thanked him, and went on up there and asked the old man for some beer.

The old man says, "Hit won't come. All my beer froze up last night."

Jack took that little rod and tapped all the barrels with it and the beer thawed and the old man was plumb tickled. So him and Jack drawed some beer and sat down and went to drinkin'.

Then Jack asked him, says, "Do you know where King Marock lives at?"

"No," says the old man, "but I know where his girls wash of a Saturday."

So he told Jack where it was, and that Saturday evenin' Jack went down to the river and through the bresh till he came to a deep pool out there one side of a cliff. There was a log there where they went in the water and Jack got over behind it and laid down in the leaves.

The girls came along pretty soon, took off their greyhound skins and laid 'em on that log. Then they went down in the water and commenced washin' around and washin' around. Jack reached up and pulled the youngest 'un's greyhound skin off the log and held on to it. They came out the water directly and the two oldest girls put on their skins and was gone, and Jack couldn't tell which way they went nor nothin'. The youngest looked around for where she'd laid her greyhound skin and couldn't find it and couldn't find it, and fin'ly Jack stood up.

"You give me my skin now."

"Take me home with you and I will."

"Oh, no, daddy would kill me."

"Take me to the gate, then."

"Oh, no, I'd be afraid to do that even, but I'll take you in sight of the house."

Jack gave her the skin and she put it on. Then she got out a solid gold needle and told Jack to take it and prick his finger on the point three times. Jack did that and the girl took him by the hand and they rose right straight up in the air and went flyin' along over the tops of the mountains. Jack had an awful good time doin' that.

Well, he saw a big house directly and the girl says to him, "Yonder it is. You better light now and come in a-walkin'."

So she went flyin' on and Jack lit. He walked on up to the gate, and there was King Marock settin' on a bench under a shade bush.

"Good evenin', King Marock."

"Oh, hit's you, is it? How'd you find me?"

"Old man told me."

"Come on in and set down."

Jack went in and he and King Marock sat there and talked till the girls called 'em to supper. They went in the house and pulled up to the table. The girls had the finest kind of supper fixed up.

Ever'thing you could think of that was good to eat was there on the boards.

"Just reach now and help yourself," says King Marock, "if you find anything you can eat. Just make yourself right at home."

Jack's mouth was just a-waterin'. He was awful hungry.

"Well, girls," he says, "your supper sure does look good. It sure Lord does!"

Time Jack said that there wasn't a thing on the table but dishwater. King Marock looked right hard at Jack and got up and left.

Then the youngest girl told Jack, says, "You mustn't ever mention the Lord around here, Jack."

Jack said he'd be sure not to do that no more, and then the girl told him, says, "He aims to kill ye, Jack, if you can't do whatever work he gives ye. Now tomorrow there'll be a thicket to clear and he'll give ye an old axe and a new one and you be sure to take the old axe. You get up before he does tomorrow mornin' and be settin' in front of the fire when he comes in."

II

Well, next mornin' Jack was up real early and had the fire goin' and was settin' there smokin' when King Marock walked in. So they cooked breakfast and eat, and then King Marock took Jack out and showed him a big thorny bresh thicket.

"Now, Jack," he says, "my grannie lost her gold ring in that field there 'fore that bresh growed up. You find that ring by tonight or I'll kill ye and put your head on a spear."

And he handed Jack two axes, an old one and a new one. Jack looked at 'em and took the new one. Then King Marock was gone and Jack went to work on that bresh, but ever' time he cut out a place it growed back twice as thick. He'd go to another place and light into it with the axe, but the same thing 'uld happen. Jack kept on hackin' away first on one side that field, then on another till the sweat just poured, and about twelve o'clock that thicket was twice as big as when he started. Then that girl came out. She had the old axe in her hand.

"How you gettin' on, Jack."

"Only fairly well," says Jack.

"What's the matter?" she asked him.

"Ever' time I cut a lick," Jack says, "hit looks like twice as much grows back up."

"Why didn't ye take the old axe, like I told ye?"

"Hit looked so rusty and brickle I was afraid it 'uld break."

Well, she handed Jack the old axe and he took it and time he'd cut three licks with it that field was plumb cleared, all but one little locust. Jack walked over to it and there was that ring on one of its branches. Jack got it off and laid that old axe there against the little tree.

"Now," the girl told him, "you stay on here till dark and then you come on in and give him the ring. Tomorrow there'll be a well to dreen and he'll give ye an old bucket and a new one, and you be sure to take the old bucket."

Jack came in after dark and handed King Marock the ring.

"You found it, did ye?" says the King. "Surely some of my people are workin' against me."

"Oh, no, there ain't," says Jack.

Next mornin' he led Jack out to an old-fashioned home-dug well, says, "Jack, my grannie's great-grannie lost her thimble in

that well and it better come out of there 'fore I get in tonight or I'll cut your head off and put it on a spear."

He handed Jack a new bucket and an old banged-up riddley one. Jack took the old bucket and saw it was full of holes, so he set it to one side and reached for the new one. And King Marock was gone from there and Jack couldn't tell which way he went.

That well-water was 'way down when Jack drawed up the first bucketful, but the more he drawed the more the water rose up, till about twelve o'clock it was runnin' out the top and all over the ground. Jack floundered around slippin' ever' which-a-way in the mud and kept on a-throwin' water till that well got to spoutin'. It like to washed Jack away from there. Then here came the youngest girl, had the old bucket with her.

"Looks like you ain't doin' so well, Jack."

Jack admitted it.

"Why didn't you take the old bucket, like I told you?"

"That old leaky thing? Why, hit's plumb riddled!"

She handed him that bucket and told him to go on and use it. Jack throwed out water with it once and all the water on top of the ground dried up. Then he dipped it in the mouth of the well and it dried up to where it was when he started in. Then he let the bucket down and pulled it up and looked and the well was dry, and there was that thimble layin' on the bottom. Jack set the old bucket there 'side the well and the girl tied a rope on him and let him down. He picked up the thimble and out he came.

"Now," she says, "tomorrow there'll be a big stone house to build out of one rock, and he'll give ye a big sledgehammer and a little rock-axe; and on the peril of your life you take the little rock-axe. You wait here till dark now, 'fore you come to the house with that thimble."

Jack waited and came on to the house about dark.

"Well, Jack, did ye find my great-great-great-grannie's thimble?"

Jack handed it to him.

King Marock he took it and sort of looked around, says, "Surely, surely, some of my people are workin' against me."

"No, there ain't," says Jack.

Next day King Marock took Jack out and showed him a big rock 'side the hill, says, "Jack, you take that rock and bust it and square up the blocks, and by the time I get in tonight you better have me a twelve-story house finished and the stone well dressed, and I want twelve rooms twelve foot square on every story, and if you don't get it all done by the time I get here I'll sure kill ye and put your head on a spear."

He handed Jack a big sledge and a little bitty rock-axe with a sawed-off handle. Jack looked up at that big rock and took the sledge and King Marock was gone.

Jack swung that big hammer and tried to block him out some stone. He hammered and he pounded and he sweated, but ever' lick it seemed like that rock just swelled a little bigger. The sweat got to runnin' off Jack in a stream and he nearly burnt the handle out of that old sledgehammer.

That girl she came out there about twelve o'clock, had the little rock-axe in her hand, says, "Looks like you've not got many stones dressed."

"No," says Jack, "seems like this rock is sort of hard to bust."

"Why didn't you take the little rock-axe, like I told ye?"

"I forgot," says Jack.

"Here," she says, and she handed it to him.

Jack hadn't struck but three licks with it when that rock just r'ared up in the air and there was a twelve-story house.

"Now," the girl told him, "when you see King Marock comin' in this evenin', you go and meet him 'fore he gets here. You take him all through that house and he'll act awful pleased, but when he gets out and turns his back on it, hit'll not be there no more. Then he'll start in cussin' you about it bein' gone, and you tell him he said for you to get it built, but there wasn't a thing in his orders about you makin' it stay built."

Jack said he'd do that, and he went to lay the little rock-axe down somewhere, but he got to lookin' at that house and studyin' about what-all he had to do, and he stuck the rock-axe in his overhall pocket.

So Jack he watched for King Marock and when he saw him comin' he went on out to meet him.

"Well, Jack, did ye get my house built?"

"Yes, sir," says Jack.

"Doors, windows, roof, and everything?"

"Yes, sir."

"How'd you do it?" the old King asked him, and he looked at Jack sort of like he suspected somethin'.

"Let's go on up there and look it over," says Jack, "so you can see does it suit you all right."

He took King Marock up to the house, and they went all through it, looked in all the rooms and how pretty they were, all fixed up just like in a ho-tel, and after a while they came on out. The old King looked up at it once more, and then he and Jack turned and started on off. Right then somethin' went off like a shot-gun behind 'em and when they looked around that house was gone. Wasn't a thing there but that same old big rock.

King Marock came up to Jack like he wanted to fight, says, "Where's my house?"

"I contracted to build it," says Jack, "not make it stay built."

Well, King Marock looked like he was about to cuss Jack out, but he just sort of shut his mouth to and walked on off a-grumblin' to himself. Jack hung around awhile and directly he went on to the house.

King Marock didn't come to the table for supper, and the youngest girl took Jack out where they wouldn't be heard and told him, says, "He'll make you take your choice of us girls tomorrow mornin', Jack. Which one will you take?"

"Why, I'll take you," says Jack.

"How'll you know us apart standin' side by side with our greyhound skins on?"

"Well, I don't know," says Jack.

"I'll lick my tongue out at ye," she says, "so you'll know that 'un is me."

Next mornin' the King didn't come to breakfast. The girls got the dishes all washed up and directly King Marock hollered for Jack.

Jack came and there stood the three girls with their greyhound skins on. Jack looked and looked, and the old King thought sure he had him that time, hollered, "Choose the youngest 'un, Jack! Pick her out quick or I'll cut your head off!"

Jack stepped back and looked at 'em again. The youngest licked her tongue out right quick, and Jack says, "This is the one, I reckon."

"All right! All right!" says King Marock, "Take her on! Take her on!"

III

And that night, after they'd all gone to bed, that girl came and woke Jack up, says, "He's done found out it was me helped you and he's a-fixin' to kill us both tonight."

"What'll we do?" says Jack.

"We'll run away," she told him. Says, "Now you go to the stable quick and bring down the horse and the mule. You better hurry."

Jack ran to the stable and there stood the sorriest-lookin' old horse and mule you ever saw, nothin' but skin and bones. The old horse's head hung so far down Jack had to prop it up to get the bridle on him. The mule was in the same fix, had his head hung 'way down in the bottom of the feed trough with his ears flopped over, and Jack had to push 'em both out the door; he had to lift their feet over the barn sill. He swarped 'em with a stick and kept on beatin' 'em and fin'ly got 'em to the house. The girl came out with saddles and bridles, a whole new outfit all shined up.

"I'll saddle 'em," says Jack.

"No," she says, "I'll saddle 'em."

She throwed the saddle on the horse and when she pulled the girth, there was as fine a ridin' horse as you'd want, slick as a ribbon and prancin' and a-r'arin' to go. Jack had to hold him down. Then she heaved the saddle on the mule and when she tightened up the belly-band, that old skinny mule filled out just as fat as his hide could hold him. Then she got on the mule and Jack jumped on the horse and they lit out.

"I can't look back now," she told Jack. "If I did he'd be able to witch us. You watch behind ye and tell me when you see him comin'."

They got on a long stretch of road directly; Jack looked back and saw King Marock a-comin'. He and the girl stopped and she handed him a thorn and told him to jump off quick and stick it in the ground behind 'em. Jack did, and all between them and the King was a big thorn thicket, locusts as big as poplars and blackberry briars big as saplin's. It was so thick a rabbit couldn't 'a got through. King Marock had to go back and find that old axe to cut him a way and by that time Jack and the girl got a good gain on him.

Then Jack looked back again, and there was the old King behind 'em, just a-tearin' the road to pieces. Jack told the girl and she stopped and handed him a little bottle of water, told him to pour that on the road behind 'em. Jack did it, and there was a wide river between them and the King. He had to go back after that old rid- dledy bucket to dreen the river off, and by that time they'd gained a right smart on him.

Jack looked over his shoulder again, and here came old King Marock a-r'arin' and a-shoutin' and beatin' his horse somethin' terrible. The girl gave Jack a little handful of gravel and told him to throw them down behind, and when Jack did that all the coun- try between them and the King was one great big rocky mountain. King Marock had to turn around and go back to get that little rock- axe to break a way through, and he hunted and he hunted all over the place for it, but he never did find it 'cause Jack had forgot and stuck it in his pocket.

So Jack and the girl rode on to the settle-ments to get married. Jack wanted to see his folks first, so they went on to his house.

"Come on," says Jack, "let's go in. They'll sure be surprised when we tell 'em."

"No," she says, "I'll not go in yet. I'll stay here at the gate awhile till you go see 'em first. Now, Jack, when you go in there don't you let any of 'em kiss you till you come out again. Don't let nothin' touch you on your lips, you hear?"

Jack said All right, and went on in. They were all real glad to see him and his mother went to huggin' him and tryin' to kiss him, but he put his hands over his face and laughed and wouldn't let her come anywhere close to his lips. Then he set down in a chair and was just about to tell 'em all about his girl when his little dog came in the door and saw Jack had come back and 'fore Jack knowed it that dog ran to him and jumped up in his lap and licked him right on the mouth. Jack put the dog on the floor, and when he tried to recollect what he was about to tell his folks he just couldn't remember a thing about that girl. She waited out at the gate quite a spell; then she guessed what must 'a happened, so she rode on off.

IV

Now there was an old shoemaker in that neighborhood, an old man and his wife and their grown girl. They were ugly as bats, all three of 'em — real homely people. That girl went and cloomb up in a bush right over the spring at this old shoemaker's house, and when his girl came to get water she peeped in the spring and saw that other girl's shadder.

"Well!" she says, "if I'm that pretty, I'll not stay here any longer." And she set her bucket down and left there to hunt her up a sweetheart.

Then the old woman she came out about the water, looked over in the spring, saw that girl's shadder in there, says, "Huh! If I'm that pretty, I'll not live with that ugly old man another minute!" So she left the water bucket standin' there and down the road she put.

Then the old man came out to see what was the matter. He looked in the spring, says, "Surely, surely, I'm not that pretty." He went lookin' around and fin'ly saw that girl up there in the tree, says, "What in the world are you a-doin' up there?"

"Restin'," she told him.

"Come on down," says the old man; "you can rest at the house."

So she came down and filled the bucket and carried it back to the house for the old man; and his old woman and his girl didn't come back, and didn't come back, so he says to that girl, "I reckon they've done left me. Do you want to hire to do my cookin' and washin' for me?"

"Yes," she says, "I'll hire."

So she stayed on there and did the old man's cookin' and housekeepin' and water-totin'.

Now Jack got to talkin' to an old sweetheart he had there 'fore he left, and pretty soon they fixed up to get married.

All the neighbors wanted new shoes to wear to the weddin' and they got to goin' to that old shoemaker. A young man came there about his shoes, and when he saw that girl he thought she was the prettiest woman he'd ever looked at. So he asked could he stay and talk with her awhile. She told him he could, and he stayed so long she commenced gettin' sleepy; but he didn't leave, and didn't leave, till fin'ly she says to him, "Would you mind coverin' the fire for me?"

He said he would, and when he started shovelin' the ashes up over the logs she slipped up in the loft.

Then she called down to him, says, "You got it covered?"

"Not yet," he told her.

"Well," she says, "your hand stick to the shovel and hit stick to you, and you set there and pat the fire till day."

So that young feller sat there a-hold of the shovel with his shins a-burnin' and kept pattin' in the ashes till daylight.

Then another young man came and — Lord! he thought she was so pretty he just had to stay and talk to her that night. He stayed on and stayed on till she wanted to go to bed.

So she got up and says to him, "Law me! There's a gander to put up. I like to forgot it. Would you put it up for me?"

He said he'd do it, and when he got the gander cornered and caught it, the girl came to the door, says, "You caught it yet?"

"Yes, I got it."

"Then you hold to hit, and hit stick to you till day."

So that boy had to stay out there all night a-holdin' on to that old gander, and it a-hootin' and a-hissin' and floggin' him with its wings, till daylight the next mornin'.

Then Jack came about his shoes, and when he saw the girl he got stuck on her somethin' awful. He kept on hangin' around till 'way up in the night. Then the girl got to gapin' and yawnin' and so she says to Jack all at once, "Oh, law me! There's a calf to pen. I surely like to forgot all about it. Would you mind pennin' it for me?"

Jack said Sure, he'd pen the calf for her, and when he got out to the calf, she hollered to him, says, "You got hold of the rope?"

"Yes," says Jack.

"Then you hang to hit, and hit hang to you, till day."

So Jack had to hang on to that rope with the calf a-bawlin' and a-pullin' and him a-hoppin' up and down and runnin' all through the mud in the barn lot all night long. Jack was sure a sight to look at when daylight broke. He came to the house and tried to wash up a little and he gave that girl a lot of money not to tell it on him. Hit 'uld not do for such a tale to get out on him and him about to get married; it would 'a ruint him.

Well, the weddin' was that next Sunday and the old man fixed up to go. He asked the girl did she want to go, but she said No, she was a stranger there and she guessed she'd stay at the house; but after the old man left, she slipped out and went on up to the church house.

Jack had just stepped out on the floor to get married when she ran her hand in her pocket and pulled out a little box. She opened it and a banty hen and rooster jumped out. Then she reached in her pocket and took out three grains of barley, threw one of 'em down and the hen got it. The little rooster ran up and pecked the hen, and the girl says, "Take care, my good fellow! You don't know the time I cleared a thicket for ye and stopped Old King Marock with all them thorn trees and briars."

Jack heard her and tried to get a look through the crowd to see what was happenin'. That other girl punched Jack to make him listen to the preacher. The preacher tried to go on, but that girl threw down another grain of barley. The little hen got it and the rooster pecked her again.

"Take care, my good fellow! You don't know the time I dreened a well for ye and stopped Old King Marock with all that water."

Jack wasn't payin' no mind to what the preacher was sayin'. Nearly ever'body quit watchin' the weddin' and crowded around that girl to see what she was doin' with her banty chickens. Then she threw down the other grain of barley for the banty hen and the rooster ran over and pecked the hen. That time even the preacher went over to see what was goin' on.

"Take care, my good fellow! You don't know the time I built a twelve-story house for ye, and stopped Old King Marock with that rocky mountain."

Well, Jack left that other girl standin' there in the middle of the floor, came through the crowd and went up to that girl, says, "Well, I guess I know somethin' about all that."

So he took her by the hand and called the preacher and he married 'em and Jack took the girl on home with him and they lived happy.

Now some folks tell it that King Marock was the Devil. I have heard the tale told that-a-way. Anyhow, even if the old King was mean and roguish, his girl was pretty smart. She made Jack a good wife.

JACK'S

HUNTING TRIPS

Back in old times there was plenty of good game back on these mountains here. And one time Jack started out real early in the mornin' on a huntin' trip. Took his daddy's old flintlock rifle down from over the fireboard, got the powder horn and some bullets, and pulled out up the river. He traveled on through the woods a right smart ways, didn't see nothin' much for a considerable long while, till first thing he knowed he looked up ahead of him, saw a deer standin' under a big oak tree — biggest deer he'd ever seen. And right over that deer was a whole flock of wild turkeys settin' on a limb. They were a-settin' up right close together in a row and the limb was pointin' right Jack's way. Jack didn't know what to do. He wanted that deer, but he wanted them turkeys too. So he got out his knife and cut the ramrod in two, put one bullet on top of the powder, then he put that half-a-ramrod in the gun and put another bullet at the top end of hit. He drawed down on the deer and when he pulled the trigger he jerked up on the gun so's the bottom bullet would go down that row of turkeys, 'lowed maybe he'd get him five or six of 'em at one shot. Well, he got the deer all right, but that other bullet struck the limb them turkeys were settin' on, split it open, and when the split clamped back together, hit clamped down on the middle toe of ever' one of them turkeys and just helt 'em there so they couldn't fly at all. Jack saw 'em a-squawkin' and a-floppin' and knowed he had them caught, so he went on over to look at his deer. Hit was a full-grown buck, had horns on him reached about six foot from tip to tip. Jack started to walk around him, saw somethin' kickin' in the bresh. Looked and found him a big fat rabbit. That bullet had gone plumb through the deer and killed a rabbit settin' in the weeds. Then Jack saw where the bullet had glanced into a holler tree. There was somethin' sticky oozin' out the hole. Jack stuck his finger in it and tasted it. Hit was sourwood honey. That holler tree was packed full of wild honey right up to the top. Well, Jack looked up at all them turkeys a-flutterin' and cluckin', and 'lowed he'd cut the limb off and take 'em home alive. So he scaled up the tree and com-menced cuttin' on that limb. When it came loose, he grabbed hold on it, but when he done that them turkeys all set in to flyin' and carried Jack on off a-hangin' to the limb. Jack was mighty near scared to death. He didn't know whether he could hold on till they stopped somewhere. Well, they kept right on up over the tops of the trees, and fin'ly Jack saw they were headed to fly right over an old stumpy tree standin' up on a ridge. So Jack said it didn't differ whether they stopped or no, he was goin' to try to drap off and light on that stumpy tree. So when they got right over it, Jack let go, but when he drapped, instead of lightin' on top of that tree, hit was holler, and Jack lit right in the mouth of the holler, went clean to the bottom. When he got up and quit staggerin' around, Jack felt somethin' come out from one side the holler and rub up against his legs. Then two more came out and got to gruntin' around and stumblin' over his feet. Jack's eyes fin'ly got used to how dark it was down there, and he saw it was three young grizzly bears.

"Bedad!" says Jack. "The old bear'll be a-comin' down in here directly and she'll eat me sure!"

He couldn't figger no way in the world to get out of there. So he had to study him some plan to try and defend himself. He'd lost his knife when he grabbed that limb. He searched ever' pocket he had, and all he could find was a old table fork with only one prong on it. Well, Jack knowed that old bear 'uld have to come down back'erds, so he decided what he'd do and he just waited and started pettin' them cubs a little. Then directly somethin' cut the light out above him all of a sudden-like and Jack heard the old grizzly bear a-scrougin' down the holler. Jumped up and reached one hand up over his head just as high as he could. And when the old bear got down close enough, Jack seized hold on her tail and com-menced gougin' her with that old table fork. The old bear went to scramblin' back out the holler and Jack he swung on tight and kept on gougin' her. When they got out at the top, Jack gave her a right quick shove and the old bear fell to the ground and broke her neck.

Jack sat there on the tree awhile and studied what he'd do next. Fin'ly he 'lowed he'd go on home and get the team to tote in his bear and his deer so he could get 'em skinned out. Well he cloomb on down and pulled out for home. Got to the river, he saw a bunch of wild ducks a-swimmin' on the near side of a bend where it was pretty deep. Jack just had to have them ducks, and he couldn't figger out how in the world he could get 'em without no gun or nothin'. He studied about it a little, then he tied the bottoms of his overhalls so's he could swim a little better, crope up and slipped in the river, kept on easin' in till he was plumb under the water. Then he went to swimmin' around under there, pulled out a long piece of string he had in his overhall pocket, and right easy-like so's not to scare 'em, he tied all the ducks' feet together. He didn't aim to let 'em fly off with him like the turkeys done, so he dove on down to the bottom and tied that rope to a big sycamore root.

Then he popped up out the water right in amongst all them ducks and they started in quackin' and a-floppin' to rise off the water, that rope 'uld jerk 'em back, and directly they were all tangled up in one bundle. Jack started wadin' out, and when he got out on the bank his pants legs felt awful heavy, and he noticed somethin' kickin' around inside 'em. He'd been down there under the water so long a bunch of fish had done got tangled up inside his old baggy overhalls. So Jack ontied his legs and kicked around till he'd shook 'em all out, and when he strung 'em up they weighed about thirty pounds. Jack slung his fish across his shoulder and picked up that passel of ducks and went on. He kept on lookin' for them turkeys, but he reckoned they'd done flown clean out the country by that time.

When he got home, Will and Tom didn't believe Jack had done all that. They hitched up the team to a big sled and took two big barrels to fetch the honey. They got the deer loaded on and Jack picked up the rabbit and throwed it on the sled 'side the deer.

Then they cut the bee-tree, and after they'd filled both barrels, the holler was still half full. Then they hauled all that back to the house, and put out after the bear. Hit weighed more'n the deer did, but they fin'ly got it loaded on. Then Will and Tom cut a hole in the bear holler and Jack caught the young'uns. They made some rope halters and tied the young bears behind the sled.

When they got out in the road again and had gone along a ways, they heard some wild turkeys a-squawkin' and there was Jack's flock still fastened on that limb and hit all tangled up on top of some bramble briars where they'd tried to light down in the bresh. Jack got him a long pole and whacked 'em all in the head to stunt 'em so's they wouldn't try to fly off no more. Then he knocked the limb loose and flung his turkeys on top of the bear.

They skinned out the deer and the bear and cured up the meat. Jack made him a couple of pens for his ducks and his turkeys, and his mother canned up all them fishes; and Jack and his folks had bear meat and deer meat and turkey meat and duck meat and fish meat to last 'em a right smart while.

Jack tamed up them young bear cubs and carried 'em down to the King's house. The King and his folks took on so over them young bears, they paid Jack a thousand dollars a-piece for 'em, They went back and got the rest of that honey too. I forget how long it was Jack eat on that honey.

II

Then there was that time I went huntin' with Jack. I had stayed all night down there, and Jack and I made it up to go out together the next mornin'. I didn't have my gun with me, but that didn't differ. We aimed to take turns with the long rifle Jack had. We went down the river a pretty far piece, and then we struck out through the woods where the timber hadn't been cut off. We didn't have much

luck, and about twelve we stopped to eat the rations Jack's mother
had fixed up for us. Jack sat down on a stump and I got up on a
big black log. I took out my bread and started eatin'. Then I opened
my knife, cut me off a chunk of meat, and jobbed my knife down
in that log. Then I noticed Jack wasn't where I thought he was.

"Where you goin', Jack?"

"I ain't goin' nowhere," says Jack. "What are you slippin' down
that log for?"

"I ain't slippin' down no log," I told him. "Why are you a-ridin'
that stump off like that?"

"This stump's right here. You're the one that's a-movin'."

Then I saw a bush come between me and Jack, so I looked
around me and I'll be confounded if I wasn't ridin' right along
through the bresh. I jumped off that log in a hurry and it crawled
on off. Hit was the biggest blamed blacksnake you ever saw.

Well, we finished our snack and went on. We fooled around
shootin' squirrels and pheasants and one thing and another. Came
out in a big pasture on top of the mountain directly and went along
the rail fence lookin' for bobwhites and turkeys and rabbits. All at
once Jack stopped, says, "Look yonder!" There set about twelve
big wild turkeys stretched out along the top of that fence.

"I wish they was all settin' on one rail," says Jack. "I might get
several with one shot."

"That's a fact," I told him. "You ain't goin' to get but one this-
a-way. Take the big gobbler on this end."

Jack didn't hear what I said. He had slipped his rifle barrel between two little saplin's growin' side by side, and was pullin' against
the stock.

"What in the world ye doin', Jack?"

"I'll show ye in a minute," he says.

Jack kept lookin' first at that fence where the turkeys were settin',
then he'd bend his gun again. Well, sir, Jack put a crook in his
gun for every crook in the fence and when he shot the ball went

zig-zaggin' down that row of turkeys and killed ever' last one. So I went and got 'em while Jack straightened out his gun.

We had a pretty good load of wild meat by that time, so we started on back. Got on down the mountain and came out in a wide swag toward the river and a big deer jumped, ran off a little ways and stopped. Jack hadn't loaded his gun and he poured some powder in right quick and reached in his pocket for a ball. Then he jerked his hand out and reached in another pocket.

"Blame it!" he says. "I'm plumb out of lead, sure's the world!"

I didn't think I had any shot with me, but I com-menced searchin' through all my pockets too. I couldn't find a thing but some peach seed where I been eatin' peaches and saved the pits to take home and plant.

Jack saw me take out a handful of 'em, says, "Hand here one of them peach rock."

He grabbed one and rammed it down in his rifle; raised up and shot. Hit that deer somewhere on the shoulder, 'cause we saw the blood fly, but the deer ran off. Then directly we jumped two more deer. It looked like a whole flock of 'em was in that swag. So Jack loaded up with another peach rock, and the next deer that jumped he tried again. *Blam!* He didn't bring it down, but we saw blood on the leaves and rocks when we went on a piece, so we knowed it had been hit all right. Well, sir, Jack kept loadin' up with peach seed and the deer kept jumpin' and Jack kept on tryin' to get one till I didn't have any peach rocks left.

Well, we were gettin' down closer to the river when all at once a big black bear came out of a laurel thicket, and 'fore we saw it hardly the blame thing r'ared up and growled and came right straight at us with its mouth wide open. Me and Jack we dropped ever'thing right there and up two trees we went, and Jack went up his little hickory saplin' so fast he cloomb six feet out the top. But he caught on a branch when he fell back in the tree and we both just waited till the old bear went on off.

Then we headed up the river, came to a little creek, and we was lookin' for a place to jump when we both noticed the water in the creek bed was movin' awful slow.

Jack got down and stuck his finger in it, tasted of it, "Honey," he says.

"No," I told him.

"Taste it," he says.

So I tasted of it, and sure as I'm a-livin' it was honey runnin' down the creek bed in the place of water. Then we noticed considerable buzzin' up the holler and we went on up that honey creek. Well, sir, ever' tree in that holler was a bee-tree. The bees were so thick you couldn't hardly see the trees and bresh. And the honey was a-drippin' and oozin' out ever'where. It ran down in little branches into that creek.

"Now, ain't that a sight in the world!" says Jack, and he leaned back on a little tree to watch the bees fly and the honey run, and when he jarred that tree something started floppin' down on the ground around us.

I picked one up and looked at it, then I smelled of it, and then I tasted of it, then I says to Jack, "Fritter!"

"Surely not," says Jack.

"Pick one up and taste it," I told him.

So Jack tried one, and don't you know there we stood in a little grove of fritter-trees. They were the best fritters you ever tasted. We shook down a mess of 'em and dipped 'em in that honey creek and eat fritters and honey till we was nearly foundered.

And just about that time we heard a racket up above us, and here came a little roast pig runnin' out the bresh with a knife and fork stuck in its back, a-squealin' to be eat. But we wasn't hungry by then, so we ran it on back.

Well, boys, Jack and me we got back in about dark, and next mornin' we divided up the squirrels and pheasants and rabbits, and Jack gave me half of his wild turkeys and I went on home.

About four years after that, Jack came to my house one day and told me, says, "You remember that swag where I shot at all them deer with them peach rock you had?"

I told him I did.

"I came through there yesterday," Jack says, "and I saw a little tree full of ripe peaches so I got to lookin' at it and a-wonderin' about peaches a-growin' out in the woods like that when I looked further up the holler and there was a lot of other little peach trees just like it. So I went on over to the first tree I saw. It was growin' up on the other side of a log and I got up on that log to pull me off a peach when all at once that tree jumped up from the ground and ran off. Then blamed if that whole peach orchard didn't rise up and run off through the woods. Them peach rock had took root in ever' deer we shot. Some of 'em had the trees a-growin' out their shoulders and some out their backs, and you remember that 'un I hit between the eyes? Well, it had a six-foot peach tree growin' right up between its horns. Hit sure was a sight in the world."

Now, boys, don't ask me too much about where it was Jack and me went huntin' that day. It was pretty far back when I was a young feller, and I can't remember exactly which way we went nor which part of which mountain that swag was in. I'd like to get some of them peaches myself.

THE HEIFER HIDE

Well, Jack's daddy had a tract of land back in the mountains, and he decided he'd give it to the boys to work. He gave Will and Tom a good horse a-piece; didn't give Jack nothin' but a little old heifer.

They went on up to that newground, fixed 'em up a pole shanty, and went to clearin' land. Jack he'd work about two hours, then he'd go back in. Will and Tom they didn't like that much. Then one day they went to work and Jack never showed up at all. So they felled a tree on Jack's heifer and killed it.

Got back that evenin', says to Jack, "You been foolin' around here and let your heifer get out. Hit came up there where we were a-cuttin' timber; tree fell on it and killed it."

"I don't much care," says Jack. "I been wantin' some beef, anyhow."

Jack went and skinned it out, left the hide pretty near whole. He salted the meat down, stuffed the hide full of shucks. Then he'd put some of the meat on a stick and roast it on the fire. Jack got fat as a pig eatin' on that beef and not workin' none, got so fat after a while you couldn't see his eyes. That beef lasted him a right smart while.

Jack was gettin' along fine, except his clothes kept bustin' — first his shirt, then his pants, and then he didn't have nothin' on at all hardly. So Jack sort of pulled that heifer hide over him. Hit was so stiff it stood right up by itself sort of like a calf, but Jack got in it some way or other, and it helped to keep him from gettin' cold.

Then one day Jack saw his beef about to give out, and he knowed he'd have to study up somethin' to do. Will and Tom wouldn't give him none of their rations on account of Jack not workin'. So, when Jack had finished the last mess of that beef, he took his heifer hide by the tail and sort of got it on him and pulled out for the low ground.

Hit was about the funniest thing you ever saw; him a-travelin' down the road with that old heifer hide by the tail and hit a-goin' fump! fump! fump! ever' step Jack took.

Well, Jack went on till it was gettin' about night, and fin'ly he came to a house, stopped and hollered, "Hello!"

Woman came to the door.

Jack says, "Can I stay the night?"

The woman looked at Jack and com-menced laughin'. "No," she says. "The man of the house ain't here."

So Jack went on, fump, fump, fump! Came to another house, hollered again. Woman came out and Jack asked her could he stop all night.

Time she saw Jack, she busted out laughin', says, "No, the man of the house ain't come back yet."

Jack went on, fump, fump, fump! Hit got plumb thick dark 'fore he got to another place. Jack got in the yard right up close to the house.

"Hello!"

The woman came out, looked at Jack, her eyes stuck out and her mouth popped open. She didn't know what in the world that thing was.

Jack says, "Can I stay the night here?"

"Oh, law, no!" she says. "The man of the house . . ."

"Blame the man of the house!" says Jack. "Hit don't differ. I got to stop somewhere."

And he went a-fumpin' right on in the house. The woman told him he could go up in the loft. So Jack went on up the stair steps, his old heifer hide fumpety, fumpety, fump! right on in behind him.

Jack sat down there, and directly he heard somebody come in. Got down on his knees and looked through a knothole in the puncheon floor; saw it was a man there dressed up awful fine, necktie stickin' out and a pretty little mustache. So he listened to what they were a-sayin', and Jack fin'ly decided that feller wasn't the man of the house.

The old woman got out all kinds of good somethin' to eat and set it on the table. That little man went to eatin' and Jack's mouth just watered. Then she put what was left back in the cupboard and got out a whole lot of good drinks. About that time somebody rode in the yard a-whistlin'.

The woman says, "Law me! That's my old man."

That little feller jumped up, says, "Where'll I get? Where'll I hide?"

"Jump in that big chest there, quick!"

So he jumped in the chest and the old lady got them drinks and all the good vittles out of sight just before the man of the house came in.

He hung up his hat, says, "Get me some supper, old woman. I'm about starved to death."

She went and got him out a little cold cornbread and cold potatoes. The man sat down and com-menced eatin'. Jack couldn't stand it no longer, so he raised up that heifer hide and rammed it against the floor. "What's that, old lady?"

"Law me! Hit's nothin' but a little old boy wanted to stay the night. He had the awfulest lookin' thing with him. I made him go up in the loft."

Man hollered up to Jack, told him to come on down. Jack came down a-draggin' his heifer hide.

"What's your name, stranger?"

"My name's Jack."

"Come on and set down, Jack. Eat a cold snack with me. Hit ain't much, but you're welcome to it."

So Jack sat down at the table, stood his heifer hide up behind him. He eat a few cornbread crusts, didn't suit him much. So he reached back and took hold on his heifer hide, churned it against the floor, made it rattle real loud, says, "You hush your mouth now. You're not to com-mence your carryin' on like that."

"What'd it say, Jack?"

"Ain't goin' to tell," says Jack. "Might make the woman of the house mad."

"Blame the woman of the house! You tell me what it said."

"Said there was all kinds of good fried ham and roast pig and chicken pie and lightbread in the cupboard yonder."

"Is there, old woman?"

"Well, now," she says, "hit's just a little I was a-savin' for my kinfolks comin' tomorrow."

"Me and Jack's your kinfolks. Bring it on out here for us."

So Jack and him eat a lot of them good rations. Jack was awful hungry, and he knowed she hadn't brought out her best stuff yet, so he rammed his heifer hide again, says, "You blobber-mouthed thing! I done told you to hush. You keep on tellin' lies now and I'll put you out the door."

"What'd it say, Jack?"

"I ain't goin' to tell ye nary other thing. Hit's done made your old woman mad already."

"Blame her, Jack! What'd it say that time?"

"Said there was some fruitcake and pies and honey and peaches in there."

"Is there, old woman?"

"Hit's just a little somethin' I was a-savin' for my kinfolks."

"Blame your kinfolks! Me and Jack's as good as them. Bring it on here."

So they eat right on. Then Jack churned his heifer hide again, says, "Confound you, Lizzie! I told you when I brought you down here you'd have to keep your mouth shut. Now I'm a good notion to take you right out of here."

"What'd it say, Jack?"

"Bedad, now! I ain't goin' to tell you no more. Your old lady's gettin' madder and madder. I'll not tell."

"Hit don't differ about her, Jack. You tell what it said."

"Said there was some good peach brandy and blackberry wine in there."

"What about it, old lady?"

"Just a little I was savin' for my poor kinfolks."

"Poor kinfolks, the nation! Me and Jack's your poor kinfolks! Fetch it on out here."

So she got the likker and put it out. Jack he took him just a common little dram. He knowed what it 'uld do for him. But that man went after it pretty heavy, till it took a right smart effect on him. He got to talkin' big, says, "Jack, what'll ye take for that thing? I'll give ye a hundred guineas."

"Law, no!" says Jack. "I can't trade my heifer hide. I might starve."

"You price it, then, Jack. I got to have it, hit don't differ what it costs."

"No," says Jack, "I can't sell my heifer hide."

"If you won't sell it to me, Jack, I'll just kill ye and take it anyhow. I got to have that thing. That's all there is to it now."

"Well," says Jack, "I'll take a hundred guineas and that old chest there."

"Oh, no," says the old lady, "not trade my chest by any means. My great-grandfather gave it to my grandfather and my grandfather gave it to my half-sister and my half-sister gave it to my second cousin and my second cousin gave it to my brother-in-law and my brother-in-law gave it to my first cousin and my first cousin gave it to me — and you ain't to sell it."

"Confound you, old woman, you and all your kinfolks! If Jack wants that chest, he can have it."

So he paid Jack a hundred guineas and holp him shoulder that chest and Jack pulled out.

He got down the road a piece and that old chest 'gun to weigh him down a right smart. Came to where there was a big well 'side the road, Jack stopped and let the chest fall, says, "You old heavy thing! I don't want ye nohow. You're a-goin' to go right down in the bottom of this here well."

"Oh, pray, Jack! Don't drop me in no well. Old Man Parsons's in here. I'll pay ye another hundred guineas not to do that."

"Bedad!" says Jack. "The blame thing's a-talkin' to me. — Let's have it then and maybe I won't do it."

So Old Parsons doubled up the money and poked Jack a hundred guineas out the crack. Jack picked up the money and pulled on down the road. That feller was so scared he forgot to trade with Jack about lettin' him out.

II

Jack got back to the newground, and when Will and Tom saw all that money they asked Jack where in the world he got it at.

"Made it off my heifer hide," says Jack.

Will and Tom says, "We'll just have to make us some money like that too."

So they went out and shot their horses and stuffed their hides with shucks.

Jack says, "You better wait till the hides cure. You may have no luck if ye don't."

"No, we'll not wait. We're a-goin' to make more money'n you did. If you can do it, we can too."

So Will and Tom pulled off all their clothes and got them horse hides around 'em and started down the road.

Well, the sun was shinin' pretty hot and directly the green flies got to blowin' around, but Will and Tom never paid no attention to that. They came to a house and hollered, "Hello!"

A woman came out and they says, "Can we stay the night?"

"No!" says the woman. "You all get on away from here! Whee-ee-ew!"

So they came to another house and hollered. A woman came out a-holdin' her nose, says, "Shee-ee-ew! Take them stinkin' horse hides away from here!"

So fin'ly Will and Tom throwed them hides in the bresh and went on back home.

"Jack, you lied!"

"No, I didn't neither."

"You did, too. We never made a cent of money. And now we're a-goin' to kill you and take your money for cheatin' us like that. You make up your mind right now, what way ye'd rather die."

So Jack says, "Well, I don't want ye to drown me."

They said to him, says, "Then that's the very way we'll kill ye."

So Will and Tom got Jack down in a hemp sack and took him on down to the river. When they got down the public road a piece, they saw they didn't have no rope to tie him.

Will says to Tom, says, "You go back to the house and get us the rope."

"No," says Tom. "You go back and get it. I'll watch Jack."

They got into such a argu-ment that fin'ly they laid Jack down in the sack and set two big logs across him, and both of 'em went back after the rope.

Jack wiggled around till he got his head out, and directly an old man came down the road drivin' a big herd of sheep.

Jack hollered at him, "Hello, uncle!"

The old man looked all around till he saw Jack, says, "Hello, stranger. What in the world are you a-doin' wrapped up in such a way as that?"

"I'm fixin' to go to heaven," says Jack. "The angels are comin' to get me just any minute now."

"Law me!" says the old man. "You look like an awful young feller. How old are ye?"

"I'm twenty-three."

"Why, you're a heap too young. I'm ninety-three. You ought to wait awhile longer. How about lettin' me get in there and go in the place of you?"

"I don't know about that," says Jack. "I may not get another chance."

"How about me tradin' you this hundred head of sheep? You let me get in there and you can have all these here sheep."

"Well, lift these logs off me, then. Hurry up. Them angels might come 'fore I can get ye fixed for 'em."

So the old man got the logs off Jack and Jack got him down in the sack head first and put the logs back like they were.

"Now, don't you say a word if the angels try to talk to ye. They'd find out it wasn't me, and they might pitch ye in the wrong place."

So Jack took that drove of sheep out of sight around a bend in the road, and sat down to wait.

Will and Tom came on back and tied the old man up, took him down to a deep hole in the river, says, "Ye got anything to say 'fore we pitch ye in?"

The old man thought they meant pitch him into heaven: never said a word. So they threw him in the river, and went on home.

They were a-countin' out Jack's money, heard somebody a-drivin' sheep up toward the yard.

"Hello! Open the gate so I can drive my sheep through."

"Who's that?" says Will.

"Sounds like Jack."

"Why, hit couldn't be Jack. We done drowned him."

So they looked out the door.

"Law me! Yes, it is Jack, too. Where in the world did he get all them sheep?"

They opened the gate and let the sheep in.

"Jack, how'd you get back here so soon, and where'd ye get all them sheep?"

"Well, boys," says Jack, "where'd you leave me at?"

"Why, we just now pitched you in the river."

"Yes," says Jack, "and if you'd pitched me ten foot further I'd 'a got another hundred head of sheep."

"You got them sheep out'n the river?" says Tom.

"Look here, Jack," says Will. "You done caused us to lose our horses, and now you got to help us get some sheep. We goin' to make you throw us in so we can have a drove of sheep too."

"Well, now," says Jack, "if nothin' else'll do ye, I'll see can I help ye get 'em. But you got to get you a couple of big sacks yourselves."

Will and Tom ran and got 'em a hemp sack a-piece and they went on down to the river.

Jack tied Will in his sack and throwed him in.

Tom saw Will a-kickin' around, says, "What's he a-kickin' for?"

"He's a-gatherin' sheep," says Jack.

"Hurry! Hurry now, Jack. Pitch me in there 'fore he gets 'em all. Throw me further'n ye did him."

So Jack went back to the newground and had him a farm and a house and all them sheep, and nobody to bother him. He took a little of that money and got him a new shirt and some overhalls, and the last time I went down to see Jack he was a-doin' well.

SOLDIER JACK

Well, Jack fin'ly joined the King's army and went off to the wars. He fought first in one country and then in another, and did pretty well. He served thirty years, and then they told him they reckoned he'd pulled his term and he could go on back home. So they gave him his dis-charge, and Jack hit the road.

Now, back in them days soldiers didn't get no pay, and all they gave a man when he left the army was two loaves of bread. Jack was a-walkin' on the highway with those loaves of lightbread stuck under his arm when he met up with a beggar, and the beggar he bummed Jack for somethin' to eat, so Jack gave him one of his loaves of bread. Then directly he met an old man with a long gray beard, and he asked Jack for some bread. Jack cut the other loaf in two and gave the old feller half of it and went on.

But he got to studyin' about that 'fore he'd gone very far, and then he turned back and caught up with the old man, says, "Daddy, I didn't do you right. I gave another man a whole loaf and I didn't give you but a half a one. Here's the rest of the loaf."

The old man thanked Jack, says, "Well, now, you're all right, Jack, and here's something I'm goin' to give you." He handed Jack a sack he had across his arm, says, "If ever you want to catch anything, you take this sack and hold it open with one hand and slap it with the other'n, and say,

'Whickety whack!
Into my sack!'

and it'll get right in this sack for ye."

Then he took a little vial out of his pocket and gave that to Jack, says, "Now, this little glass will tell you whether somebody who's sick will die or get well. All you got to do is fill it up with clear spring water and look through it. If you see Death standin' at the foot of the bed, that person'll get well, but if Death is waitin' at the head of the bed, you'll know they're about to die."

Jack thanked the old man and went on with the sack over his shoulder and the glass in his pocket. He traveled on and traveled on, and along toward night the road went through a woodland and Jack heard some turkeys cluckin'. Looked up in a big oak tree and there set nine wild turkeys. So Jack opened the sack and slapped it, says,

"Whickety whack!
Into my sack!"

—and all nine of them turkeys flew right down and got in the sack. Jack pulled the mouth of the sack together and went on. He came to a town about dark, went to a ho-tel and asked could he swap his turkeys for a room and somethin' to eat. The ho-tel missus she weighed the turkeys and Jack got a room and supper and breakfast and a little change to boot.

Next day Jack went on, and about twelve he passed by a big fine house near the road, looked like nobody lived there. The yard was growed up in weeds and there wasn't no curtains in the windows, and Jack got to wonderin' about such a good house bein' empty. Met a boy in the road directly and the boy told Jack the house was ha'nted. Jack asked who did the place belong to and the boy told him. So Jack went down to that man's house and got to talkin' to him about it.

"Yes," the man told him, "that house has been ha'nted for thirty or forty years. There can't nobody stay there overnight. I've promised several fellers that if they'd stay all night up there I'd deed 'em the house and a thousand acres and give 'em a thousand dollars, but there ain't nobody ever broke the ha'nt yet."

"I'll try it," says Jack. "I'll stay there all night."

Well, that man took him up on it and they got some grub for Jack to eat while he stayed there, and the man took Jack on to the house and holp him build up a fire and then left him there. Jack sat down by the fire and got out his pipe and smoked awhile. Then he fixed his supper and eat it and lit up his pipe again and sat right on tendin' his fire ever' now and then and a-waitin'. Well, it got up 'way on in the night, and about midnight Jack heard a great roar and somethin' knockin' around upstairs and wheels a-rollin' and chains a-rattlin', and then three little devils came jumpin' down the stair steps. Jack sat right on. The little devils had some sacks of money with 'em and they came over to the fire and com-menced banterin' Jack for a poker game. Jack didn't have no money except that change from the ho-tel, but he sat down and invested it, and got to winnin' off the little devils. They lost ever' time, and started tryin' to peep and see Jack's hole card, but he was slick and played close to the floor, and it wasn't long till he cleaned 'em out. Then they got mad and went to fussin' at Jack and threatenin' him with great swoards, and so Jack picked up that sack and held it open, says,

*"Whickety whack!
Into my sack!"*

and all three of them little devils scrouged right down in the sack. Jack pulled the mouth of the sack to and tied it, put it in one corner and then he laid down by the fire and went to sleep.

Next mornin' the man came back, and there was Jack cookin' his breakfast. Jack told him what happened and showed him the sack full of devils, so that man deeded Jack the house and the thousand acres and paid him a thousand dollars, and then they took the little devils down to the blacksmith shop and hired the blacksmith to sledge 'em for twenty-four hours. "I want you to lay the hammer to 'em," Jack told him. So he did that, and it was a sight

how the sparks flew. There wasn't a thing but ashes in Jack's sack when that blacksmith got done. So Jack paid him and took the sack on home and put it up on the fireboard.

Well, Jack fixed up the house and hired boys to help him tend the land and he lived on there by himself and took it sort of easy. He was gettin' to be an old man, Jack was, and he didn't work too hard. He enjoyed lookin' after ever'thing and makin' little improvements around his place; but he had plenty of money, so he hired most of the heavy work done and lived right on there and saw to it that the boys made the crops pay pretty well.

Then one day word came down in that settle-ment that the King's girl was down sick and all the doctors were lookin' for her to die. They said she couldn't be cured, so the King had all the doctors' heads cut off. Then the King he put out word that anybody could cure his girl, he'd pay 'em several thousand dollars.

Well, Jack he didn't want the money, but he thought he'd go up there and see about that girl. So he got down his sack and stuck that little glass vial in his coat pocket and went on to the King's house. The King took him in where his girl was a-lyin' in the bed and Jack sent for some clear spring water. They brought it to him and he filled up that little vial, held it up and looked through it, and there was Death standin' at the head of the bed, grinnin'. Jack set the vial down and got his sack opened up, struck it with his hand, says,

> "Whickety whack!
> Into my sack!"

—and Death got down in the sack. Jack tied the sack up tight, and the King's girl got well, and they brought the money to Jack, but he wouldn't take it. Then Jack went on home, and he had one of the boys take that sack and tie it 'way up in the top of a big poplar tree standin' there in the yard.

Well, Jack kept on with his place and his house. The boys who worked for him, they'd grow up and get married and go off and he'd hire some others. He noticed his hair was grayin' up considerable and he growed him a beard directly and it com-menced gettin' sort of long, but Jack he enjoyed life and never paid much attention to the almanac. He kept a calendar so he could tell when it was Sunday and not work, but he never noticed what year it was. He stayed at home by himself most of the time, didn't get out much to go anywhere.

Then one spring mornin' Jack decided he'd take a walk over in the settle-ment, see friendly faces and have a little pleasure talkin' to people. He got down the road a piece and met up with an old lady. Jack looked at her and he never had seen anybody as old as she was. Her face was so wrinkled and leathery it was terrible to look at. Her eyes set 'way back in her head and her white hair was so thin it was almost gone. She was stooped over so her nose almost bumped her knees when she walked.

Jack stopped, says, "Howdy do, ma'm."

She started straightenin' up, with her bones a-crackin' and her head a-shakin' like palsy, and fin'ly she got her eyes up where she could look at Jack.

"Howdy do, son," she says.

"How you gettin' on, granny?" Jack asked her.

"Oh, law, son," she says, "it's awful."

"Why, what's the matter, granny?" says Jack.

"Matter?" she says. "Why, livin' as long as this, that's what it is."

"Yes," Jack says, "you do look sort of old-like. Just how old are ye, ma'm?"

"Next June," she says, "on the twelfth day of the month, I'll be two hundred and six years old."

"Well, I declare!" says Jack. "I never did hear of anybody gettin' to be that old."

"It ain't right," says the old lady, "livin' that long and not bein' able to die."

"You mean you want to die?"

"O Lord, yes," she told him.

"Well, why can't ye die, granny?"

"Why, ain't you heard?" the old lady asked him. "Some fool's got Death shut up in a sack. There ain't nobody died around here for a hundred and forty-two years, and you know that's against nature, now ain't it?"

Jack turned around right there and went on back home. He studied about what the old lady said for a day or two, then he called one of his boys to climb up in that poplar tree and bring him down the sack was up there. The boy cloomb up and brought the sack in to Jack. Jack took his knife and cut the sack where he'd tied it, and when Death got loose, all the old folks com-menced droppin' dead wherever they was. And Jack was about the first one Death got, I reckon.

APPENDIX AND

PARALLELS

by Herbert Halpert

APPENDIX

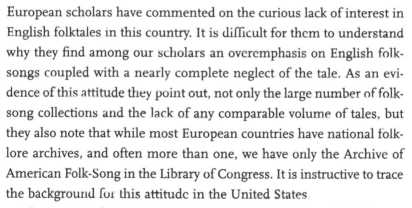

European scholars have commented on the curious lack of interest in English folktales in this country. It is difficult for them to understand why they find among our scholars an overemphasis on English folksongs coupled with a nearly complete neglect of the tale. As an evidence of this attitude they point out, not only the large number of folksong collections and the lack of any comparable volume of tales, but they also note that while most European countries have national folklore archives, and often more than one, we have only the Archive of American Folk-Song in the Library of Congress. It is instructive to trace the background for this attitude in the United States.

The nineteenth century witnessed a tremendous growth of interest in the folktale in Europe, especially after the appearance of the *Household Tales* of the Grimm brothers in 1812. Literary men and scholars in nearly every European country went out into the highways and byways to collect songs and tales from the lips of the peasants. This was the period when the great European folktale collections were made: in

Russia, in Norway, in Highland Scotland, and elsewhere. While the scholars were preoccupied with the problems of the origin and diffusion of European tales, literary men in Europe self-consciously worked with folk materials, seeking to get closer to the national spirit.

In the United States in the nineteenth century, the folktale had a vital relationship with literature, but it was not a self-conscious one. The tall tale formed the basis, as Professors Blair, Meine, and others have shown us, for a large section of the regional literature of the South and West. Tall tales have long been assumed to be a peculiarly American form, but somehow not worthy either of collection or serious study. From the early days of this country they flourished mightily in travelers' tales describing the marvels of a new continent. Benjamin Franklin parodied such tales by pretending to give an authentic description of the magnificent leap of the whale up Niagara Falls in pursuit of codfish, "esteemed by all who have seen it as one of the finest Spectacles in Nature." Such stories have always fitted in with the bravado and humor of our many frontiers. No doubt such yarns were often produced by the active imaginations of the story-tellers; but they were in imitation of a rich oral lore, in turn solidly rooted in the tradition of northwestern Europe. *The Travels of Baron Münchausen,* published in England in 1785, had a great influence on our oral tale, but its tales were originally taken from the German.

Story-telling in the nineteenth century was not limited to the rural settlers. Lawyers on circuit swapped yarns. Best known of them was a young country lawyer, Abe Lincoln, who carried the practice to the White House. All through the early part of the century there was a constant interchange between oral and printed lore by way of the newspapers and almanacs. Through these means folklore worked into the regional writers. The study of the effect of this folklore on literature is quite recent with American literary historians, and they have given little notice to the European relationships of the tall tale. They have been occupied primarily with the literature it helped to generate.

From the folklorist's point of view it was the Negro's contribution in tale, as in song, that first received attention in the United States. This came through Joel Chandler Harris's *Uncle Remus* stories which appeared in 1880, charming literary adaptations of tales told by English-speaking Negroes. But though folklorists were interested and a few similar collections appeared, it did not give rise to any considerable body of work.

On the other hand, ballad hunting became, and still is, a recognized scholarly sport. In part this was due to the discovery that folksongs were still sung in the United States. In large measure, however, we may attribute this activity to the prestige that Harvard, and the Harvard tradition of ballad scholarship, had in academic circles. This had its origin in the great editorial work of Francis James Child, whose compilation, *The English and Scottish Popular Ballads*, became accepted as a scholarly canon. After Child's death, George Lyman Kittredge and his students dominated folklore studies in the United States, and perhaps unconsciously took the attitude that the disciples could do no better than to carry on in the master's footsteps. This has led to a certain aridity in folkloristic activity in this country and a formalized and restricted range of interests.[1]

Not till the founding of the American Folklore Society in 1888, with its publications, the *Journal of American Folk-Lore*, and the Memoir series, did the longer folktales of the English-speaking white settlers get any attention. A few English folktales appeared in the early volumes of the *Journal*. Until a few years ago this handful represented nearly all that there was to show.

Although the English folktale languished unnoticed, other folktales did not suffer the same fate. The anthropologists proceeded to collect

---

1. (See note on page vii of Preface.) The work of the Society founded in 1911 by the late Cecil Sharp: "to preserve English folk dances, songs [*ballads* incl.], and music . . . ; to include related American forms; to make them known, and to encourage their practice . . ." — has done much to make the approach to these traditions less acidly academic. — R. C.

and study Indian myths and tales until at present no part of the world has been covered as systematically and as well. The anthropologists did more. It was largely through the guidance of Franz Boas that the American Folklore Society encouraged the recording of French and Spanish tales on this continent, and lengthy contributions in the *Journal* attest that these efforts met with success. The collection of Negro folktales was also stimulated, and these later garnerings, coming some thirty-five years after Uncle Remus and continuing to the present, were more broadly inclusive than the earlier ones. Elsie Clews Parsons and her fellow workers found that the Negroes had adopted, not only the tall tales and "noodle" stories of the whites, but that Negroes in this country, in Nova Scotia, and in the West Indies also knew the longer European folktales.

The discoveries of the anthropologist did not seem to affect the literary scholars. It is possible, however, that we may ascribe to still another cause their lack of interest in the folktale. Although both Ireland and Scotland had fine collections of the longer tales that are common all across Europe — the kind misleadingly called "fairy tales" — no comparable collections have been made in England. The two compilations by Joseph Jacobs are reasonably large, but he was forced to use material from chapbooks and ballads, and to draw on stories from Lowland Scotland, Australia, and America to eke out the number. As contrasted with the richness of ballad material in both England and America, no doubt the field seemed meager and promised small rewards.

There were a number of questions that troubled folklorists. Why was there, both in England and this country, this comparative scarcity of a kind of tale known over the rest of Europe? Was England an exception to the European area and had such tales always been rare there? Had they come over to this country, but for some reason died out and perhaps become moribund in England? Or — had these tales simply missed the boat and never come over? Since they had existed in England, even though to an undetermined extent, the folklorist felt they should have been found in America along with the ballads. For the folklorist in a way is a scientist: in some measure he too works by prediction. He would expect to find folktales here, just as surely as he would expect to find "Barbara Allen" and "Lord Randall" known in any area where English folksongs are sung.

So to the folklorist the satisfactory thing about Mr. Chase's discoveries which we have in this volume is that they show the folklorist was right. The tales were here for someone who knew how to seek them out. Mr. Chase is not the first collector to find them. In addition to the tales which appeared long ago in the *Journal of American Folk-Lore*, several smaller groups have been published within the last twenty years by Emelyn E. Gardner, Bertha McKee Dobie, Ralph Steele Boggs, and Isobel Gordon Carter. But Mr. Chase's collection more than doubles the largest of these, and together with other still unpublished material, he has more than all of them put together. The richness of his collection will henceforth make it much easier for other collectors to know what to ask for, since they will know what is in oral circulation. We may confidently look forward to having many of these tales found elsewhere in the United States.

In April, 1939, while I was recording folklore for the Library of Congress, I was fortunate enough to get a number of these Jack Tales from Sam Harmon in Tennessee. Just the previous month I had been collecting folksongs in Wise County, Virginia, and near-by Letcher County, Kentucky, and never thought to ask for tales. About a year later, Mr. Chase worked in the same area and with some of the same informants from whom I had recorded songs — and got tales from them. I intrude this personal note to draw a very obvious moral: to get folktales you must ask for them. Perhaps that is the reason that so few have been recorded up to this time. Exercising the folklorist's bent for prediction, I would suspect that with a little effort more of these tales could also be found in England.

Mr. Chase deserves considerable credit for tracing the folktales in one family tradition. The discovery of the interrelationship of the Ward-Harmon-Gentry families is a fine achievement. It becomes increasingly clear that the most significant results for the future in folklore will come, not from the big collections that skim material from here, there, and everywhere, but rather from those devoted to limited areas, single families, and even single individuals. It is only in this way that we will get a picture of just how folktales fit into their social setting. I have failed to ask Mr. Chase whether the Wards know folksongs. It is worth noting that both Mrs. Jane Gentry and Sam Harmon were singers with remarkable repertories.

Another of Mr. Chase's significant contributions is his recognition of the importance of "Jack" as the central figure in this British-American tradition. "Jack" appears also in Jacobs's English collection. He is not necessarily English in character; Irish collectors have pointed out with some surprise that "Jack" figures largely in the Irish tradition, even among Gaelic-speaking story-tellers.

Miss Martha Beckwith, whose letter Mr. Chase quotes, makes the very good point that "Jack" is a kind of trickster-hero, one who is successful through his cleverness. Certainly he is not the admirable prince of fairy tales, but rather a quickwitted and not always too scrupulous farm boy. While such a hero is definitely part of the northwestern European pattern, what should be stressed is that in these stories he is the *only* central figure.

It is hard not to interpret the very direct symbolism in the heroes people use in their tales and legends. We realize a little uncomfortably that in these tales as told in the Southern mountains "Jack" is an ordinary poor boy who achieves success only in one of two ways: either by his wits, or by sheer luck—and the latter method predominates. Here we have an almost mocking contradiction of what has been called "the American fairy tale"—that honesty and hard work are the means to success. It is difficult to know just how much of this is the conscious reflection of an attitude toward our society on the part of the story-tellers. Sam Harmon remarked to me: "If I was to name my boys over, I'd name all of them 'Jack.' I never knowed a Jack but what was lucky." His tone in saying this was only half jesting.

I think the trickster aspect of "Jack," together with these psychological implications, is at least in part, the reason these tales have appealed so extensively to English-speaking Negroes. They have adopted him, along with the tales, and sharpened his trickster character even further. The conclusions we might draw from folklore on the stresses and conflicts in Negro life can be confirmed from the reports of students of the social sciences. Negroes, of course, have adapted many white traditions to their own cultural patterns, not merely taken them over.

A final observation that might be made is on the use of one character as the central figure in this cycle of stories. I have mentioned that, before Mr. Chase, no one had noticed that these longer folktales had a central figure. On the other hand, the cycle form is not only world-wide, but has taken many varied forms in American folklore. We have the legendary giants, such as Paul Bunyan and Peco Bill; the strong men, like Antoine Barada of Nebraska, Joe Call of New York, and the recently discovered Bobby Hayes of Indiana; the trickster, like "Boney" Quillin of New York, who is the center of "true" anecdotes; and perhaps most popular, the Munchausens, such as John Darling of New York and "Oregon" Smith of Indiana. Mr. Chase has added "Jack" to this goodly company.

The tales in this collection are not documentary transcriptions. Mr. Chase has rewritten them for children and has explained his procedure in making composites. His chief interest has been in bringing folklore into usable form and thus attempting to preserve its spirit rather than the exact letter. In doing this he is in the tradition started by the Grimm brothers and followed by Joseph Jacobs in England. We can be grateful that, like his distinguished predecessors, he regards the folk tradition, not merely as literary material, but as the stuff of knowledge. For the scholars, therefore, he has noted carefully just what changes he has made from the original text.

Though these texts cannot be used in studying the native story-telling style, materials for studying this style can be found in Miss Isobel

Gordon Carter's article which has stories taken down literally from a member of this family.[2] Furthermore, at some future date I hope to publish an exact transcription of my own recordings of Sam Harmon. Many of us will hope that whatever slight loss there is to the specialist will be more than made up by the greater appeal these artistic recreations will have for the general public.

To add to the scholarly usefulness of this work Mr. Chase had me add the parallels which follow his notes to each of the stories. I have given references to the classic Grimm tales by number. These tales can be read conveniently in Margaret Hunt's translation of the *Household Tales*. Jacobs's English and Celtic collections are also referred to by number because the pagination varies in the different editions. I have noted the occurrence of these tales in Sir George W. Dasent's delightful translations from Asbjörnsen and Moe which make available to English readers other material from northwestern Europe.

Since nearly all of these tales are represented in Grimm, full European, and indeed world-wide, parallels down to about 1918 will be found in Bolte and Polívka's exhaustive annotations. I have given the type numbers of these tales according to the Aarne-Thompson Type-Index. Professor Stith Thompson was kind enough to aid me in this. Since most of the unpublished folktales in the European folklore archives are indexed according to this system, this furnishes an additional key to the distribution study of these tales. The Type-Index lists many of these archive references.

I have taken most pains with the English, Irish, Scotch, and American parallels. We do not as yet know just what the sources of English folktale in America are, but it may be assumed that it is one of the first three or some combination of them. I have added full references to Negro texts in English, since many of them no doubt stem from English sources. These references largely supplement Bolte and Polívka for the British Isles, the West Indies, and the United States.

---

2. See native writing style given in notes to No. XIII. — R. C.

Many books and journals are given abbreviated references after their first use in these notes. I have also saved space when referring to articles after the first time[3] by giving just the author's last name and the journal reference, except for Miss Carter's article which is referred to only by page.

Herbert Halpert
INDIANA UNIVERSITY
December 31, 1942

---

3. See, especially, notes to No. III. — R. C.

PARALLELS

1. Jack in the Giants' Newground

Sources: R. M. Ward, Martha Ward Presnell, Roby Hicks, Ben Hicks.

Parallels. This story combines a number of well-known types often found separately or in various other combinations: Type 1088, *Eating Contest* (A. Aarne and S. Thompson, *The Types of The Folk Tale*, Folklore Fellows Communications No. 74, Helsinki, 1928); 1060, *Squeezing the (Supposed) Stone;* 1640, incident III (a), getting giants to kill one another by striking them from ambush; 1045 (or 1049), *Pulling the Lake Together;* 1063, *Throwing Contest with Club;* 1121, *Ogre's Wife Burned in Her Own Oven;* 328, incident II (a), threatens giant with army — locks him up to protect him. Many of these incidents are often found in combination with Type 1640, *The Brave Tailor.*

As might be expected the closest parallel is that in Carter *(Journal of American Folk-Lore,* XXXVIII, 1925), pp. 351–54. A number of the combined incidents are in J. F. Campbell, *Popular Tales of the West Highlands,* II, 328–32, 342–43; Sir G. W. Dasent, *Popular Tales from the Norse,*

No. V. Many of them are given as part of Type 1640, in Béaloideas, The Journal of the Folklore of Ireland Society, IV, 253; VII, 68–69; D. Hyde, *Beside the Fire* (London, 1910), pp. 3–15; also see Beal. X, 100, which has further references. Two Negro texts also have several of these incidents combined with Type 1640: Parsons, *Bahamas, Memoirs of the American Folk-Lore Society,* XIII, 133–35; and E. C. Parsons, "Barbados Folklore," JAFL XXXVIII (1925), 273. Jacobs, *English,* No. XIX, has Types 1088, and 328, II (a). J. Jacobs, *More English Fairy Tales* (New York and London, n.d.), No. LVIII, has Type 1640, III (a). For Type 1121, see Beal. II, 15, and consult Bolte-Polívka for further references. Type 1060 occurs in Boggs, JAFL XL VII, 309; Hyde, p. 175; and Jacobs, *Celtic,* No. XVIII.

Type 1063 seems to be popular with American Negroes. In Fauset, JAFL XL, 250, it is combined with other giant-tricking incidents. It is given as an independent story in: J. M. Brewer, "Juneteenth," PTFLS X (1935), 50–51, Z. N. Hurston, *Mules and Men* (Philadelphia and London, 1935), pp. 197–98; E. C. Parsons, "Folk-Tales Collected at Miami, Fla.," JAFL XXX (1917), 223; Writers' Program of the Work Projects Administration, *South Carolina Folk Tales (Bulletin* of University of South Carolina, October, 1941), pp. 80–81. In these versions the angels in heaven are warned to "move over." (H. H.)

Remarks: Wards' title "Jack and the Giants." Minor omission made by editor in cut paunch episode.

2. JACK AND THE BULL

Sources: Mr. and Mrs. James Taylor Adams, Finley Adams, Mrs. Nancy Shores, Mrs. Polly Johnson; all of Wise County, Virginia. My first knowledge of this tale came through James Taylor Adams.

Parallels. This is a combination of Type 511, *One-Eye, Two-Eyes, Three-Eyes,* and Type 530, *The Princess on the Glass Mountain;* the bull as the animal helper is probably a form of Type 314, or part of the Cap o' Rushes theme, Type 510.

I cannot find complete parallels to this tale. The bull helper with the ear "cornucopia" is in Jacobs, *More English,* No. XL VIII, and No. LXXIX has a bull-calf helper whose bladder helps kill a dragon. See also Beal. II, 268–72 (and a list of versions on p. 273); IV, 310–11; Dasent, *Norse,* No. I. In Beal. VII, 46–47, a belt from the bull's skin obeys orders and ties giants. In Fauset, *Nova Scotia,* MAFLS XXIV, 41–43, there is a belt and a stick which obey orders and kill giants and a dragon.

Parsons, *Bahamas,* MAFLS XIII, 27–28, combines the bull-calf and horn cornucopia with Type 511. An Aberdeenshire text in *Folk-Lore Journal,* II (1884), 72–74, has a calf helper and evil sisters. There are texts of Type 511, in Beal. VII, 243; Campbell, *West Highlands,* II, 300–06; M. R. Cox, *Cinderella (Publications of the Folk-Lore Society,* XXXI, London, 1893), pp. 534–35; E. C. Parsons, "Tales from Guilford County, North Carolina," JAFL XXX (1917), 198. See also: Grimm, No. 130; Bolte-Polívka, HI, 60–66. For Type 530 sec: Bolte-Polívka, III, 111–14; Dasent, *Norse,* No. XIII. (H. H.)

Remarks: Mrs. Polly Johnson had a fragmentary episode concerning the King setting up a greased plank beside a pole on top of which was a golden ball. Jack gets the ball and the King's girl knows him in spite of his rags when this golden ball rolls out of his pocket.

I am indebted to Mrs. Eudora Ramsay Richardson, State Supervisor of the Virginia Writers' Project, for permission to use materials concerning this tale and Nos. XV and XVIII.

3. JACK AND THE BEAN TREE

Sources: R. M. Ward, Ben Hicks, Roby Hicks, Mrs. Martha Lethcoe of Damascus, Virginia.

Parallels. This tale is best known in the Australian text J. Jacobs gives in his *English Fairy Tales* (New York, 1893) No. XIII. "Jack and the Beanstalk" seems to be an almost uniquely British form of Type 328, *The Boy Steals the Giant's Treasure.* The general European versions do not have the beanstalk episode. In the United States the story is popular in the Harmon-Ward family tradition. Miss Isobel Gordon Carter secured it from Mrs. Jane Gentry, of Hot Springs, North Carolina ("Mountain White Folk-Lore: Tales from the Southern Blue Ridge," *Journal of American Folk-Lore*, XXXVIII (1925), 365–66), and in 1939 I recorded it from Sam Harmon, near Maryville, Tennessee, for the Library of Congress. It has also been found among English-speaking Negroes. See: E. C. Parsons, "Tales from Maryland and Pennsylvania," JAFL XXX (1917), 212–13; E. C. Parsons, *Folk-Tales of Andros Island, Bahamas* (*Memoirs of the American Folk-Lore Society*, XIII, Lancaster, Pa. and New York, 1918), p. 133; M. W. Beckwith, *Jamaica Anansi Stories* (MAFLS XVII, New York, 1924), p. 149. There is a moralistic English chap-book version reprinted in E. S. Hartland, *English Fairy and Other Folk Tales* (Camelot Series, London, n.d.), pp. 35–44.

The Scotch and Irish forms of this tale do not have the beanstalk, and usually have a clever girl who steals the giant's wonderful possessions. See Jacobs, *English*, No. XXII; J. F. Campbell, *Popular Tales of the West Highlands* (Paisley, 1890–92–93), I, 259–74; Béaloideas, The Journal of the Folklore of Ireland Society, II, 10–12 (and bibliography on p. 23); III, 348–49; L. L. Duncan, "Folk-Lore Gleanings from County Leitrim," *Folk-Lore* IV (1893), 184–88; J. Jacobs, *More Celtic Fairy Tales* (New York and London, n.d.), No. XXXIX — reprinted from Jeremiah Curtin's articles in the *New York Sun;* P. Kennedy, *Fireside Stories of Ireland* (Dublin and London, 1870), p. 3 ff.

G. W. Dasent, *Popular Tales from the Norse* (London and New York, n.d.), pp. 240–45, gives a delightful English translation ("Boots and the Troll") from the great Norwegian collection of Asbjörnsen and Moe. For further European parallels see J. Bolte and G. Polívka, *Anmerkumgen zu den Kinder-und Hausmärchen der Brüder Grimm* (Leipzig, 1913–18), II, 511 ff.; III, 33–37, and consult the references under Type 328. (H. H.)

Remarks: Ben Hicks's version had the usual cow in the first part, but I gathered that this was brought home from school by one of his children who had read it in his reader. Ben's giant said, "I smell the blood of an Irishman." Wards' title the same. On the second trip Jack usually steals a colt or a heifer. "Scat there!": R. M. W. actually said, "See-cat, there!"

4. JACK AND THE ROBBERS

Sources: R. M. W., Elisha Rasnik, Wise County, Virginia.

Parallels. This is Type 130, *The Animals in Night Quarters*, most familiar from Grimm, No. 27, "The Bremen Town-Musicians." See Bolte-Polívka, I, 237–59, and the study of the tale by A. Aarne, *Die Tiere auf der Wanderschaft* (FFC XI). For a translation from the Norwegian of Asbjörnsen, sec G. W. Dasent, *Tales from the Fjeld* (New York, n.d.), pp. 283–88.

The tale seems to be better known in the United States than in Great Britain. The version given in Jacobs, *English*, No. V, is taken from one of three American texts presented in JAFL (1888), 227–33. See also R. S. Boggs, "North Carolina White Folktales and Riddles," JAFL XLVII (1934), 294; B. Mck. Dobie, "Tales and Rhymes of a Texas Household" (Publications of the Texas Folk-Lore Society, VI, 1927), pp. 33–37. Negro versions are given in A. H. Fauset, "Negro Folk Tales from the South," JAFL XL (1927), 258; and in Parsons, *Bahamas*, MAFLS XIII, 135.

The tale has been found in Scotland (Campbell, *West Highlands*, I, 199–207), and Ireland (P. Kennedy, *Legendary Fictions of the Irish Celts*, London, 1866, pp. 5–12, reprinted in J. Jacobs, *Celtic Fairy Tales*, New York and London, n.d., No. XIV; Beal. I, 94), but I have found no report of it from England. (H. H.)

Remarks: Wards' own title. Mr. Rasnik called the tale "Jack and the Rogues." The bull is from his version which also had a swarm of bees and a flock of geese.

5. JACK AND THE NORTH WEST WIND

Sources: R. M. W., Ben Hicks.

Parallels. This is Type 563, *The Table, the Ass, and the Stick*. See Grimm, No. 36, Bolte-Polívka, I, 349–61; Dasent, *Norse*, pp. 250–53. It has been studied by Aarne in the *Journal de la Soc. Finno-Ougrienne*, XXVII (1909), 1–96. The tale in Jacobs, *English*, No. XXXIX, is one of two variants which S. Baring-Gould contributed to the first edition of W. Henderson, *Notes on the Folk Lore of the Northern Counties of England and the Borders* (London, 1866), pp. 327–31. Irish versions are given in Kennedy, *Fireside Stories*, pp. 25–30; and [T. C. Croker], *Fairy Legends and Traditions of the South of Ireland* (London, 1834), pp. 33–45.

In North America we find the story in Carter, JAFL XXXVIII, 363–65; Dobie, PTFLS VI, 45–47; and A. H. Fauset, *Folklore from Nova Scotia* (MAFLS XXIV, New York, 1931), pp. 33–35, 41–42. Negro texts are in Parsons, JAFL XXX, 210–12; Z. Hurston, "Dance Songs and Tales from the Bahamas," JAFL XLIII (1930), 307–09; Parsons, *Bahamas*, MAFLS XIII, 141; Beckwith, *Jamaica*, MAFLS XVII, 31–33. The magical objects and animals vary quite considerably in the different versions. (H. H.)

Remarks: Wards' own title. In the Norse tale the old man is the North West Wind himself. R. M. W. calls him "Jack's uncle." Ben Hicks says, "an old man." This character seems a little like The Stranger in "Fill Bowl," and in "Hardy Hardhead."

6. Jack and the Varmints

Sources: R. M. W., Miles A. Ward, Ben H., George Trivett.

Parallels. This tale is also in Carter, pp. 355–57, and I recorded it in Tennessee from Sam Harmon. It is a version of Type 1640, *The Brave Tailor,* though it lacks the giant episodes, such as those in the previous story, with which it is frequently found in conjunction. See Grimm, No. 20; Bolte-Polívka, I, 148–65. Also see: Jacobs, *More English,* No. LVIII; Beal. IV, 253; VII, 68–69; Hyde, pp. 3–15; Parsons, *Bahamas,* MAFLSXIII, 133–35; Parsons, JAFL XXXVIII, 272–74; H. Zunser, "A New Mexican Village," JAFL XLVIII (1935), 158–59. Compare with this story the curious tale in J. Curtin, *Hero-Tales of Ireland* (Boston, 1911), pp. 140–62, in which a man kills several wild animals and giants through strength, not trickery.

For the trick of getting a dangerous beast locked into a house or church see: Fauset, *Nova Scotia,* MAFLS XXIV, 98; W. Larminie, *West Irish Folk-Tales and Romances* (London, 1898), p. 78. There is a humorous Negro tale of the coward who runs from a bear and pretends he is bringing it in alive to save trouble; see: Brewer, PTFLS X, 35–36; Fauset, *Nova Scotia,* MAFLS XXIV, 66–67; Fauset, JAFL XL, 271. (H. H.)

Remarks: Wards' title "The Lion and The Unicorn." The rhyme on Jack's belt, as given by all our informants, had to be altered for printing.

7. BIG JACK AND LITTLE JACK

Sources: R. M. W., Roby Hicks.

Parallels. This is Type 1000, *Bargain Not to Become Angry,* combined with Type 1007, *Killing Live Stock,* Type 1011, *Tearing up the Orchard,* and a form of Type 1563, *"Both?".* I recorded a version of this from Sam Harmon. For references on Type 1000, see Bolte-Polívka, II, 293–94. For the combination of Types 1000 and 1007, see: Beal. IV, 253; VI, 44–47; X, 178–80; Campbell, *West Highlands,* II, 318–43; Kennedy, *Fireside Stories,* pp. 74–80, reprinted in Jacobs, *Celtic,* No. XX. For Type 1000 also see Fauset, *Nova Scotia,* MAFLS XXIV, 38–40. For Type 1007, see Beal. X, 175. (H. H.)

Remarks: The title is from Roby Hicks.

8. SOP DOLL!

Sources: R. M. W., Jane Gentry (per Carter).

Parallels. This witch tale is also in Carter, pp. 354–55, and is extremely common in British-American tradition. For very full lists of parallels, see: A. Taylor, *Modern Philology,* XVII, 59, note 8; Gardner, *Schoharie,* p. 74 and note 139; H. Halpert, "Indiana Storyteller," *Hoosier Folklore Bulletin,* I (1942), 60–61. (H. H.)

Remarks: The phrase "Sop doll!" is puzzling. R. M. W. says he thinks "doll" means "paw." When Marshall Ward tells this tale his "Sop doll-ll!"

sounds more like "sop darr-rr!" with a high inflection on the "sop." Wards'
own title, "The Silver Knife" is from a Virginia version of this tale.

9. JACK AND THE KING'S GIRL

Source: R. M. W.

Parallels. This is a form of Type 571, *Making the Princess Laugh,* combined with Type 1696, *"What Should I Have Said (Done)?"* For the combination of the two stories, see Jacobs, *English,* No. XXVII, and Chambers, pp. 101–03. For Type 571, see: Grimm, No. 64; Bolte-Polívka, II,
39–44; Jacobs, *Celtic,* No. XXVI, cited from Kennedy, *Legendary Fictions,* pp. 23–31; Kennedy, *Fireside Stories,* pp. 103–13. Two Negro texts
are in Fauset, JAFL XL, 248–49; Parsons, *Bahamas,* MAFLS XIII, 128.

For Type 1696 see: Grimm, No. 143; Bolte-Polívka, III, 145 ff.; Dasent,
Fjeld, pp. 358–75; Beal. III, 44–46 (see for further references); Kennedy,
Fireside Stories, pp. 30–33; Kennedy, *Legendary Fictions,* pp. 39–42; Jacobs,
More English, No. LXXXIV. In the United States see: JAFL III (1890),
292–93; Dobie, PTFLS VI, 54; and a Negro text from Virginia in A. M.
Bacon and E. C. Parsons, "Folk-Lore from Elizabeth City County, Vir-
ginia," JAFL XXXV (1922), 307–08. (H. H.)

Remarks: Wards' title "Lazy Jack."

10. FILL, BOWL! FILL!

Source: R. M. W.

Parallels. This is Type 570, *The Rabbit-herd.* See: Grimm, No. 165, incident C; Bolte-Polívka, III, 267–74; Dasent, *Fjeld,* pp. 1–14. This tale
has been recorded by Carter, pp. 350–51; E. G. Parsons, *Folk-Lore of the
Sea Islands, South Carolina* (MAFLS XVI, Cambridge, Mass., and New
York, 1923), pp. 102–03; Zunser, JAFL XLVIII, 161–64. Without the sack
of lies incident the story is in R. Chambers, *Popular Rhymes of Scotland*
(London and Edinburgh, 1870), pp. 103–05. The tricking of the king and
his family is in a story in Parsons, *Bahamas,* MAFLS XIII, 150.

This interesting type of tale, which has prose interspersed with song is called a *cante fable*. The form has rarely been reported from English-speaking Whites in America, as I point out in my brief study "The Cante Fable in Decay" *Southern Folklore Quarterly*, V (1941), 191 ff., although the form is quite old in both the European and African storytelling traditions — and even further east. Mr. Chase deserves congratulations for his recovery of such a rare item. In a note to "Childe Rowland," in Jacobs, *English*, pp. 242–43, Mr. Jacobs suggests that "all folktales of a serious character" originally took this *cante fable* form. This example, and those I have presented in "The Cante Fable in New Jersey," JAFL LV (1942), 133–43, are far from being of a "serious" character — though I may be misinterpreting Mr. Jacobs's use of the word. (H. H.)

Remarks: The most unusual feature of this tale and of *Hardy Hard-head* is the Woden-like character of the old man. The appearance of the god Woden (Odin, the Norse god for whom Wednesday, Wodens-day, was named) as Old Graybeard, The Stranger, The Wanderer (as in Wagner's *Ring*) occurs six times in the Volsunga Saga: 1, as a stranger at Sigmund's wedding, with a long cloak, broad hat, and magic sword; 2, as an unknown ferryman, to Sigmund bearing Sinfjotli's body; 3, as a stranger who breaks Sigmund's sword in battle; 4, as an old man with a long beard to Sigurd who does not know him; he helps Sigurd choose his horse from the herd by driving them toward the river where only Grani swims across; this appearance with its dialogue is closest to our story here; 5, as a stranger standing on a headland, to Sigurd whose ships are storm-driven; when he is taken on board the storm subsides; 6, as an old man with a long gray beard, to Sigurd when he is digging the trench to carry off Fafnir's blood. There is also an appearance in The Prose Edda: as a poor old man who invites Hrolf Kraki and his men to stay at his hut. — I had known this phase of Woden's character from my childhood as well as from a later reading of both the Prose Edda and The Poetic Edda. I must say that it was rather a surprise finding the Old Man on the slopes of Beech Mountain, North Carolina — R. M. W. in telling this tale always makes quite a point of the stranger's foreknowledge of Jack's adventures, and of Jack's surprise that the old man should know his name. — The point of singing the bowl full *of lies* seems to have been lost in the Ward-Harmon tradition. Doctor Stith Thompson cleared up this point for the present editor who restored it here. R. M. W. had said simply, "sing the bowl full." (R. C.)

11. HARDY HARDHEAD

Sources: R. M. W., Mrs. Grover Long.

Parallels. This is Type 513 B, *The Land and Water Ship.* There is a text of this in Carter, pp. 346–49, and I also recorded it from Sam Harmon. See: Grimm, No. 71, and part of No. 165; Bolte-Polívka, II, 79–96; III, 267–74; Dasent, *Fjeld,* pp. 341–52; Dasent, *Norse,* No. XX; Campbell, *West Highlands,* I, 244–47; J. G. McKay, *More West Highland Tales* (London, 1940), pp. 49–61; D. MacInnes, *Folk and Hero Tales (Waifs and Strays of Celtic Tradition, Argyllshire Series,* II, London, 1890), 53–67, and see note on p. 445 ff.; J. MacDougall, *Folk and Hero Tales (Waifs and Strays,* III, London, 1891), pp. 2–9; Curtin, *Hero Tales,* pp. 182–97, 438–62; J. Curtin, *Myths and Folk-Lore of Ireland* (Boston, 1890), pp. 270–80; Hyde, pp. 19–47. For Negro texts see: A. H. Fauset, "Tales and Riddles Collected in Philadelphia," JAFL XLI (1928), 537–40; Parsons, *Sea Islands,* MAILS XVI, 130–31; Parsons, *Bahamas,* MAFLS XIII, 32–35. There are *three* helpers in Beal. II, 194; VII, 63–64; Jacobs, *More Celtic,* No. XLIII. (H. H.)

12. OLD FIRE DRAGAMAN

Source: R. M. W.

Parallels. This is Type 301 A, *The Three Stolen Princesses.* For references and analysis see: Beal. VIII, 97–99; Bolte-Polívka, II, 300–18; Parsons, *Bahamas,* MAFLS XIII, 142, note 1. See: Grimm, No. 91; Beal. IV, 423–24; V, 209–10; XI, *Supplement,* pp. 14–24 (reprinted from J. Curtin's articles in the *New York Sun);* Curtin, *Hero Tales,* pp. 262–82;

Kennedy, *Legendary Fictions*, pp. 43–53; Campbell, *West Highlands*, I, 244–51; III, 9–32; S. O. Addy, *Household Tales with other Traditional Remains* (London and Sheffield, 1895), pp. 50–53. There is a text in Carter, pp. 341–43. The eating scene is given in Parsons, *Bahamas*, MAFLS XIII, 143. (H. H.)

Remarks: This rather unusual tale seems to be quite extant among our people: in Kentucky, Sally Middleton's "Little Black Hunchety Hunch"; in Carmen, North Carolina, The Shelton Family's "Little Nippy"; in Damascus, Virginia, Mrs. Lethcoe's untitled tale where Jack goes down to three successive "other worlds" to find each of the pretty girls; in Wise County, Virginia, Cecil Riser's "Jack and Old Tush." In Zora Neale Hurston's book of folklore from Florida Negroes "Mules and Men," and in the North Carolina "Little Nippy," the boy gets back to the upper world by riding on a buzzard's back.

At first glance this tale's connection with "Beowulf" would seem rather far-fetched. However, the hero does descend to "another world" to battle a monster; and in one Virginia version I heard him described as a "slimy, slobbery old hairy man" who lived down under the water. In the second part of the Anglo-Saxon epic the monster's name is "Fire Drake," although the similarity of this with "Fire Dragaman" may be merely coincidental. In this regard Martha Warren Beckwith has written me as follows:

"Panzer believes that the Beowulf epic is based on the folktale of the 'Bear's son,' whose story is familiar to us in Grimm 91, where 'Hans' is 'youngest-best.' In Kennedy's *Fiction of the Irish Celts*, 39–48, 'Seven Inches' is 'youngest-best' in a version of the same story, etc. Panzer has eight or nine pages of references to the Bear's son folktale. Beowulf — Bee-wulf — i.e., Bear, because of the bear's fondness for honey, but the Beowulf figure does not correspond exactly to the 'youngest-best' since he retails the prodigies of valor which he has already achieved. I do not know if Panzer's study has been accepted as conclusive, but his folktale parallels seem all well taken. Your Old Fire Dragaman is certainly a variant of the same story." (R. C.)

13. Jack and the Doctor's Girl

Sources: R. M. W., Ben H.

Parallels. This is Type 1525 A, *The Master Thief.* See: Grimm, No. 192; Bolte-Polívka, III, 379–406; Dasent, *Norse,* No. XXXV; Jacobs, *More Celtic,* No. XXVIII, taken from Kennedy, *Fireside Stories,* pp. 38–46. See also: Campbell, *West Highlands,* I, 330–64; II, 253–78; McKay, pp. 119–29; Beal. II, 11, 348–51, 359 (has Irish references); V, 78; VII, 64, 72–75; VIII, 224; X, 165–72 (reprinted from *The Royal Hibernian Tales*) and additional references on p. 201. Two Negro texts are in Brewer, PTFLS X, 15–16; Parsons, *Bahamas,* MAFLS XIII, 11–12. (H. H.)

Remarks: Wards' own title. Ben Hicks has "opium" instead of "chloryform" and doesn't mention the drugstore. It is a lynched nigger in all the Ward tellings, not a scarecrow. A version of this same tale is told by Porter Boone who lives near White Top Mountain at Kennarock, Virginia. His title for it is "Jack The Thief."

Frank Proffit, who lives near Beech Creek, has a different version of this same tale which he has written out as told by his father, Wiley Proffit. As an example of one of these tales being written down by a native tale-teller we print Frank Proffit's tale herewith:

Copied by Anna Hicks Presnell from Frank Proffit's copy written by him from the telling of his father Wiley Proffit. Punctuated, in part, by R. C.

Jack Tale

Jack and his mother worked for a old rich man for their Living. Jack he found out where the old rich man Kept his money and he concluded he would steal it. So he got two more fellers to go with him. Jack says, "I'll go in and get the money and if they wake up and find me out, I'll whistle and you'uns can get away."

So they went to the old rich man's house and Jack he went in and opened the burroh drower and he found so much gold and silver that he went to patting his foot and whistling. The two fellers on the out side thought he was warning them and a way they ran as fast as they could go. So Jack he got all the money and went home with it.

So Jack didn't go down to work for the old rich man for two or three weeks. So the old rich man went to see what had became of him. Jack was gone when he got there, and he asked Jack's mother why Jack hadn't been down to work. She says, "We are just as independent as you are." He says, "Why?" She says, "My son Jack has be come a high way robber." "He is?" And while he was there Jack comes in. He says to Jack, "Jack, they say you have be come a high way robber." He says, "Yes." The old rich man says, "There's one thing you must do between now and tomorrow morning or I'll have you hung or shot certain." Jack says, "What's that?" He says, "You got to steal my sadle horse to night or I'll have you hung or shot certain tomorrow morning." Jack says, "If I do is it mine?" And the rich man said "Yes." So that night the old rich man Locked the door and Placed two gards at the stable door. So the gards built them up a big fire and laid at the stable door.

Along about mid night along came a old ragged man a Limping along. He said to the gards that he had traveled so far that he wanted to Lay down by the fire and rest til morning. So the gards told him he could. The gards laid awake and watched him. The old man Laid down by the fire and lay there. After while he turned over and pulled out a bottle of rum and let on like he was taking a Dram, and set it down by his head. When he went to snoring again one of the gards said, "That 'uns mine." So he got it and drunk it. After while they seen the old man turn over and reach for his bottle of rum and couldn't find it, so he run his hand in his pocket and pulled out another bottle and turned it up like he was taking a dram and placed it by his head. The other gard says, "That one is mine" and he drunk that and in a short time they didn't know nothing they was so drunk. So Jack he got up when he seen they was drunk and hunted in their pockets and got the key and un locked the door and taken the horse out and put the bridle and saddle on and locked the door back up and put the key back in the gard's pocket and got on the horse and away he went.

The old rich man come out the next morning to the stable. "My horse is here, is he?" he said. "Yes, here's the key." The old rich man

unlocked the door. "My horse is gone," he said. "I gray Jack's got him."
He went up to see Jack. "Jack, you got my horse, did you?" "No sir, not
yours but mine."

The old man says, "There's another thing you've got to do again tomorrow morning or I'll have you hung or shot certain." Jack: "What's
that?" "You've got to steal all my Brother Dickie's money or I'll have you
hung or shot tomorrow morning." Jack says, "'Fi do, is it mine?" "Yes."

They was a meeting house purty close to Brother Dickie's, and away
in the night Brother Dickie heard preaching going on in the church
and there wasn't no appointment of any meeting so he went up and
knocked on the door and says, "Who's this?" And Jack says, "It's the
angel gable." [Gabriel.] And he says "What can I give you to be in thy
place?" And Jack says, "All thy money and you can be in my place."
And Brother Dickie says, "I'll go and get it then." So he started on after
it and Jack he got down and slipped a long be hind Brother Dickie and
when he got home his wife asked him who that was up there a preaching. He told her it was the angle gable. "And he said I could Be in his
place for all my money." She says, "Just take half the money. He won't
know the difference." Jack he run back and got in the stand and was
preaching when Brother Dickie got back. He knocked on the door and
says, "Here's all my money. Let me be in thy place." He says, "Not all
thy money, it's only Just half. Go get the other and you can be in my
place." So Brother Dickie goes back after the rest of the mony and Jack
slippes along to lissen. When he got there he says to his wife, "It is the
angle gable sure enough. How did he know I Just got half the mony?"
She says, "Just take it all and go on to heaven. I'll soon be there too."
Jack hurried on Back and was up in the stand a preaching when here
come Brother Dickie. Knocked on the door and said "here's all my
money. Let me be in thy place." Jack says, "all right. get me a big sack
to take you to heaven in." So he got it. He tied it up hard and fast and
he got him on his shoulder and carried him to the pen where the old
rich man kept his fattening hogs and put him in among the fattening
hogs. The old rich man went down the next morning Bright and early

to his Brother Dickie's and asked his wife where his Brother Dickie
was. His wife says "The angle gable come Last night and took him to
heaven for all his money." He says, "I gray Jack got it." He went on
Back home and By that time the sarvants had went out to feed the hogs.
They seen the sack in there wiggling around and got scared and run
Back. They told the old man. He went out and untied it. Out crawled
his Brother Dickie!

He went up to see Jack. "Jack you got my Brother Dickie's mony did
you?" "No. not his'n but mine."

"Well, there's another thing you've got to do or I'll have you hung
or shot certain." "What's that?" "You've got to steal my 5 hundred head
of cattle and put them in your pasture or I'll have you hung or shot to
morrow morning." "If I do are they mine?" "Yes."

That night the old rich man had his hands to start with the cattle to
another pasture. Jack killed him a sheep and got him a bladder of blood
and run on a head and stripped his self nacked and hung his self over
the road by the hill and Put the Blood on his face. The drivers come
up and the cattle got scared and run into the woods. The drivers is
scared too but they git the cattle together again and goes on. Jack cuts
hisself down and run ahead and hangs hisself over the road again, by
the heels. The drivers comes up again. They get scared bad that time
and the cattle run off in the woods. But they finally gets the cattle together again and goes on. Jack cuts his self down again and runs ahead
again. The drivers come up again. That time it scares them so bad that
they run off and leaves the cattle. Jack gathers the cattle up, and takes
them and puts them in his pasture.

Next morning the old man comes over and sees the cattle in Jack's
pasture. "Well you got my cattle Last night did you?" "Not yours but
mine."

"Well they's another thing you've got to do or I'll have you hung or
shot certain." "What's that?" "You've got to steal my wife's shimmy off
her back or I'll have you hung or shot to morrow morning." "If I do,
is it mine?" "Yes."

That night the old man sat by his bed with his gun, watching the window.

Jack knew of a man that was burried the day Be fore. He goes and digs him out and kills a sheep and gets him a Bladder of Blood and goes to the old man's window and raises the Dead man's face up to the window and pulls it back, raises it up again and pulls it back. The next time "Key Bang" goes the gun. Jack drops the dead man and bustes the Bladder of Blood on his face and hides. The old man comes out and sees the dead man laying there with the Blood on his face. He goes back and tells his wife, "Well, I've killed the rascal. I'll get two of my trusted Best friends to help me bury him and will be shet of the rascal, and no one will know nothing about it." When the old man is gone, in a little while Jack goes in and gets in the Bed with the old woman. Jack could talk like the old man. "Well, we won't have to be bothered with him no more." "I'm glad of it," says the old woman.

"I'll swear," says Jack, "if I didn't for get to wash after handling that old rascal, and I got blood all over your clean shimmy." "That's all right. While you are washing there in the pan I'll put me on a clean one." Jack lets on like he's washing. "Here, lay the shimmy over there," says the old woman. Jack picks it up and puts it under his arm and away he goes.

After while the old man come in. "That's a good job done," he says. "Well, wasn't you here a little while ago?" she says. "No." "Well, some one come in and I thought it was you and said he got Blood all over his hands and he got it all over my clean shimmy. I pulled it off and he went away with it." "I gray Jack got it."

Next morning the old man went over to Jack's house; "Well, you got my wife's shimmy last night did you?" "Not hers but mine."

"Well there's one more thing you've got to do. If you do it I'll give you a deed to half of my farm. If not I'll have you hung or shot certain. You've got to come to my house in the morning nether riding walking Hopping scipping nor jumping. Neather come in nor stay out. Or I'll have you hung or shot certain."

Next morning Jack caught him a old sowe and went from one side to the other with one foot touching. When he got to the old rich man's house he comes out and opened the gate and said "Come in." Jack he just straddled the gate, didn't go in or stay out.

The old man give him a deed to his farm so Jack was now richer than the old rich man.

Writin by Anna Presnell
BEECH CREEK, N.C.

14. CAT 'N MOUSE!

Sources: R. M. W., Miles A. W., Marshall P. Ward.

Parallels. This seems to be a version of Type 401, *The Princess Transformed into Deer.* This tale seems to be quite rare; Carter, p 349, has the only variant in English that I have been able to locate. See Bolte-Polívka, II, 335–48. Spending three frightful nights in a castle is also part of Type 400. It should be observed that there are many stories in English in which spending a night in a haunted house brings a reward to the courageous guest.

It is a necessary precaution, as is well known, that when you have a witch in your power, you never give her anything unless you want to let her have her freedom. (H. H.)

Remarks: The function of the talking fox in this tale is not quite clear. Possibly some parts of the story have been lost in oral transmission.

15. JACK AND KING MAROCK

Sources: Mrs. Nancy Shores and Gaines Kilgore, of Wise County, Virginia.

Parallels. This is Type 313 C, *The Girl as Helper in the Hero's Flight.* See Grimm, Nos. 113, 193; Bolte-Polívka, II, 516–27; Dasent, *Norse,* No. XI; A. Aarne, *Die magische Flucht* (FFC 92, Helsinki, 1930); R. Th. Christiansen, "A Gaelic Fairytale in Norway," Beal. I, 107–14. This is a very widely known tale but I have found no report of it from England.

For Irish texts see: Beal. I, 273; II, 19–23 (and references on p. 25), 189; III, 31–35; V, 138; VII, 243; VIII, 224; IX, 132; XI, *Supplement*, pp. 25–34 (reprinted from J. Curtin's articles in the *New York Sun*); Jacobs, *More Celtic*, No. XXXIX; Curtin, *Hero Tales*, pp. 163–81; Curtin, *Myths*, pp. 32–49; Kennedy, *Fireside Stories*, pp. 56–63; J. Britten, "Irish Folk-Tales," *Folk-Lore Journal*, I, 316–24; L. McManus, "Folk Tales from Co. Mayo, Ireland," *Folk-Lore*, XXVI, 191–95; P. G. Brewster, "Folk-Tales from Indiana and Missouri," *Folk-Lore*, L, 294–96 (and pp. 296–97 for references. Tale secured in Missouri but originally learned in Co. Limerick, Ireland).

There are Scotch texts in Jacobs, *English*, No. VII; Campbell, *West Highlands*, I, 25–63 (one of these is the chief source for Jacobs, *Celtic*, No. XXIV); MacInnes, *Waifs and Strays*, II, 1–31.

The only White text from America is given by W. W. Newell, "Lady Featherflight," JAFL VI (1893), 54–62 (see for references). There are a number of Negro texts. See: M. Beckwith, *Jamaica*, MAFLS XVII, 135–39; Edwards, *Bahamas*, MAFLS III, 99–100; M. Emmons, "Confidences from Old Nacogdoches," PTFLS VII, 128–30; Fauset, *Nova Scotia*, MAFLS XXIV, 7–9; Hurston, pp. 70–77; Parsons, JAFL XXXV, 280–81; XXXVIII, 275; XLI, 490–92, 504, 506–07; Parsons, *Bahamas*, MAFLS XIII, 54–60; *Folk-Lore Journal*, I, 284–87 (quoted from "Monk" Lewis's *Journal*).

For the incident of the devil's daughter as a helper, but no magic flight, see Parsons, *Sea Islands*, MAFLS XVI, 52–53. For the incident of the kiss causing forgetfulness, see A. W. Trowbridge, "Negro Customs and Folk-Stories of Jamaica," JAFL IX (1896), 284–85. For the incident of the chaste wife who puts her lovers in an embarrassing position, see Jacobs, *More English*, No. L; Beal. VII, 61; Kennedy, *Legendary Fictions*, pp. 63–64. (H. H.)

Remarks: Gaines Kilgore's tale is called "Willie and the Devil." Mrs. Nancy Shores told all of Gaines's tale, but carried it far beyond the pursuit, where Gaines's tradition ended. An instance of the persistence of these tales in the traditions of a family occurred in Pittsburgh recently. I told a Jack Tale at a meeting of students and teachers of the Department of English of the University of Pittsburgh; and after the lecture a student came up and asked me if I had ever heard "Jack and King Marock"! It turned out that she had heard it from her grandmother, who was a sister to Mrs. Shores, and that these sisters had been separated since early childhood. (R. C.)

16. JACK'S HUNTING TRIPS

Sources: Part I: R. M. W., Miles A. Ward, Roby Hicks. Part II: Clate Baldwin of White Top, Virginia; Tom Peters of Norton, Virginia; Johnny Martin Kilgore of Wise, Virginia; and Boyd Boiling of Flat Gap, Virginia.

Parallels. Part I. Forms of *The Wonderful Hunt,* Type 1890, often combined with forms of Type 189S, *A Man Wading in Water Catches Many Fish In His Boots,* are among the most popular of American tales. I have collected full references in my notes to versions of the tale in the *Hoosier Folklore Bulletin,* I (1942), 20–21, 41–42, 53–54, 91–92. We also have here Type 1900, *How the Man Came Out of a Tree Stump,* for which there is a North Carolina parallel in Boggs, JAFL XLVII, 315.

Part II. This combines several popular American yarns. Variants of the story of the snake that appears to be a log are in *South Carolina Folk Tales,* p. 108; G. Anderson, "Tennessee Tall Tales," *Tennessee Folklore Society Bulletin,* V (1939), 60 and 61; Halpert, *Hoosier Folklore Bulletin,* I, 49–50. I have also collected versions of this tale in New Jersey, New York and Pennsylvania.

There are many versions of a story of bending a gun so it will shoot around a hill, but Mr. Chase's form of the story seems to be unique.

The peach tree deer is a version of the Münchausen tale of the tree growing from the head of a deer shot with cherry seeds. I have given an Indiana text and American references in H. Halpert and E. Robinson, "'Oregon' Smith, an Indiana Folk Hero," *Southern Folklore Quarterly,* VI (1942), 165. Add: *Hoosier Folklore Bulletin,* I (1942), 101. In the *Tennessee Folklore Society Bulletin,* I (1935), 11, mention is made of a tree growing from the side of a bear shot with peach seeds.

The last section of the story belongs to Type 1930, *Scharaffenland*, the land in which impossible things happen. See: Grimm, Nos. 158, 159; Bolte-Polívka, III, 244–58. There is a fine version of this tale in G. B. Johnson, *John Henry* (Chapel Hill, 1929), pp. 144–45. The pigs, with knife and fork in their backs, crying, "Who'll eat me?" is an opening formula for a tale in Beal. III, 31. For its use as a closing formula in a folk play, see M. Campbell, "Survivals of Old Folk Drama in the Kentucky Mountains," JAFL LI (1938), 24. (H. H.)

Remarks: Part H has been adapted and added to Mr. Ward's *Jack Tale* by the editor. The honey creek, fritter-trees, and roast pig squealing to be eat, are from Boyd Boiling's long tale "The Forks of Honey River at the Foot of Pancake Mountain."

17. THE HEIFER HIDE

Sources: R. M. W., M A. W., Ben H., Stanley Hicks, Mrs. Grover Long.

Parallels. This is Type 1535, *The Rich and the Poor Peasant.* See: Grimm, No. 61; Bolte-Polívka, II, 1–18; Dasent, *Norse,* No. XLVII. Seamus O'-Duilearga, who lists Irish references in Beal. X, 202, says this tale is one of the most widely-known and most popular of all Irish folk-tales. He thinks there is a clearly marked influence on the oral versions from the chap-book text (*The Royal Hibernian Tales*) which he reprints in Beal. X, 184–86. See: Beal. IV, 253; VIII, 87; Kennedy, *Fireside Stones,* p. 98 ff.; K. W. Michaelis, "An Irish Folk-Tale," JAFL XXIII (1910), 425–28 (collected in Massachusetts from an Irish maid who had recently immigrated); Jacobs, *Celtic,* No. VI; Campbell, *West Highlands,* II, 232–52.

In America the story is reported by Carter, pp. 343–46; Boggs, JAFL XLVII, 308–09; E. E. Gardner, *Folklore from the Schoharie Hills, New York* (Ann Arbor, 1937), pp. 177–80 (with references and discussion on pp. 180–82); Fauset, *Nova Scotia,* MAFLS XXIV, 1–5 (see p. 1, note 1 for additional references). There are Negro texts in Hurston, pp. 64–68; Fauset, JAFL XL, 253–55; E. C. Parsons, *Folk-Lore of the Sea Islands, South Carolina* (MAFLS XVI, Cambridge, Mass., and New York, 1923), pp. 69–71; Beckwith, *Jamaica*, MAFLS XVII, 141–44, 164. Incomplete forms of the story are in J. B. Andrews, "Ananci Stories," *Folk-Lore Record*, III, 54–55; C. L. Edwards, *Bahama Songs and Stories* (MAFLS III, New York, 1895), pp. 95–96 (reprinted from JAFL IV, 248–49); E. G. Parsons, "Folk-Lore from Aiken, S.C.," JAFL XXXIV (1921), 14; Fauset, *Nova Scotia*, MAFLS XXIV, 35–36.

Raising the devil by lighting tow in a barrel is a feat ascribed to the noted preacher, Lorenzo Dow. See Gardner, *Schoharie*, pp. 37–38, 314–17. (H. H.)

Remarks: Jack's age varies considerably in the Wards' tellings. Mostly he is a boy about sixteen. R. M. W. had him say "twenty-three" once in answer to the old man with the sheep. In Wise County, Virginia, this tale is called "Fool Jack and The Talking Crow": Jack swaps his cow hide for a crow. Instead of the chest episode, the old man hides in a barrel of wool; and Jack makes his crow "raise the devil" when he lights the wool through the bung-hole. (R.C.)

18. SOLDIER JACK

Source: Gaines Kilgore.

Parallels. This is a mixture of Type 330, *The Smith Outwits the Devil*, and Type 332, *Godfather Death*. For Type 330 see: Grimm, Nos. 81, 82; Bolte-Polívka, II, 149–63, 163–89; Dasent, *Norse*, No. XVI; Beal. VII, 243; X, 160–65 (additional Irish references on p. 20); XI, *Supplement*, pp. 45–49 (reprinted from J. Curtin's articles in the *New York Sun*); P. Ussher, "Waterford Folk-Tales," *Folk-Lore*, XXV, 230–31; Fauset, *Nova Scotia*, MAFLS XXIV, 80. For American Negro texts, see Emmons, PTFLS VII, 130–32; J. G. Harris, *Uncle Remus, His Songs and His Sayings* (New York, 1885), No. XXXII; A. W. Whitney and G. C. Bullock, *Folk-Lore from Maryland* (MAFLS XVIII, New York, 1925), pp. 181–83. For the incident of pounding the devil in a knapsack see Campbell, *West Highlands*, II, 290–95; J. Macdougall and G. Calder, *Folk Tales and Fairy Lore in Gaelic and English* (Edinburgh, 1910), pp. 31–32; Dasent, *Norse*, No. LIII.

For Type 332 see: Grimm, Nos. 42, 44; Bolte-Polívka, I, 377–88; Dasent, *Fjeld*, pp. 108–15; Beal. II, 110 (and additional Irish references on p. 111); Macdougall and Calder, pp. 69–73. (H. H.)

Remarks: The version given here was edited from an unusually good recording of the tale from Gaines Kilgore by James Taylor Adams, and from the editor's own field notes of several recordings from the same informant. (R. C.)

Early editions of the following *Jack Tales* were printed in *The Southern Folklore Quarterly* as follows:

Jack in the Giants' Newground, Vol. 1, No. 1.

Jack and the Varmints, Vol. 1, No. 4.

Jack's Hunting Trip, Vol. 2, No. 3.

Fill, Bowl! Fill! Vol. 3, No. 1.

Old Fire Dragaman, Vol. 5, No. 3.

GLOSSARY

BLUBBERS: bubbles.

BOBBLE: "make a bobble": pull a boner.

BOOMER: small red mountain squirrel.

BOOT: "something given in addition to equalize an exchange." Webster.

BRESH: brush, undergrowth.

BRICKLY: brittle.

CALL FIGURES: call out directions for country dance figures.

FIREBOARD: mantelpiece.

GUINEA: an English coin once used in America.

HAND-SPIKE: a small wooden crowbar.

HIT: it. Generally used to strengthen the pronoun's definiteness.

JENNY: a female donkey.

LIGHTS: "window lights"—window panes.

MELT: milt, the spleen.

NEWGROUND: fields cleared of trees and undergrowth and culti-vated for the first time.

PAINTER: panther, mountain lion.

PIGGIN: an old-fashioned wooden bucket.

PIZEN: poison.

POKE: sack.

PUNCHEON: a heavy hand-hewn board.

QUERLED: coiled.

QUILED: coiled.

RIVIN': riving. To rive — to split a block of wood into flat pieces with a tool called a froe.

SHADDER: shadow, i.e. (in *Jack and King Marock*), reflection.

SHET, "GET SHET OF": get rid of.

SWAG: a little glen or hollow depression on the side of a mountain.

TURN, "TURN OF MEAL": this means simply the amount of corn carried to the mill where one waits his turn to have his corn ground.

USIN', "WHERE THE HOG WAS A-USIN'": "hanging around" is the slang equivalent. This sense of the word generally refers only to animals.

WHIPLIN': whistling.